Claiming Skyler
Shifter Series, Book 2

By

Jaden Sinclair

Published by
Melange Books, LLC
White Bear Lake, MN 55110
www.melange-books.com

Claiming Skyler ~ Copyright © 2009-2015 by Jaden Sinclair

ISBN: 978-1-61235-028-8

Names, characters, and incidents depicted in this book are products of the author's imagination or are used fictitiously. Any resemblance to actual events, locales, organizations, or persons, living or dead, is entirely coincidental and beyond the intent of the author or the publisher. No part of this book may be reproduced or transmitted in any form or by any means, electronic or mechanical, including photocopying, recording, or by any information storage and retrieval system, without permission in writing from the publisher.
Second Edition

Cover Artist: Caroline Andrus

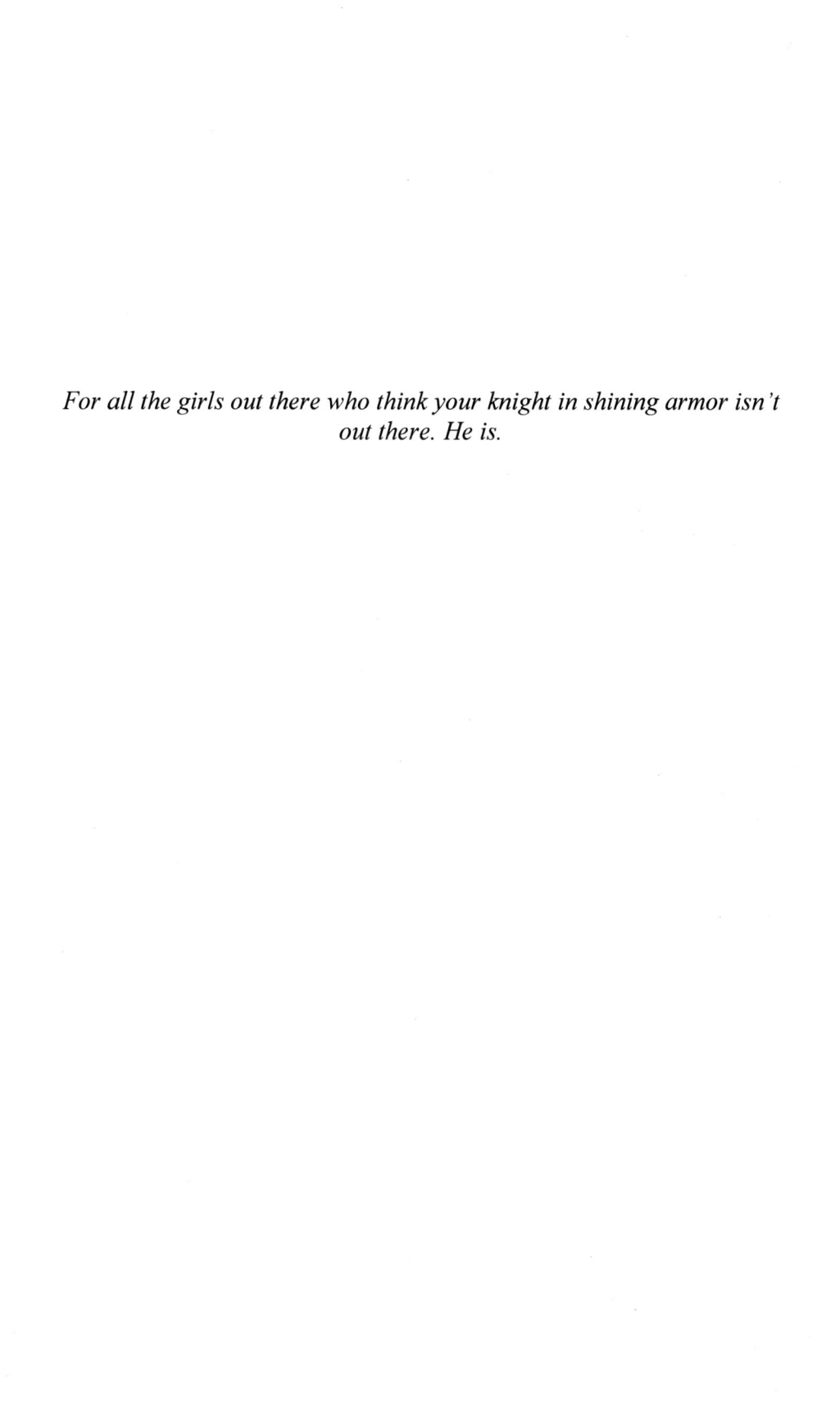

For all the girls out there who think your knight in shining armor isn't out there. He is.

Chapter One

Adrian Laswell drove down the long, gravel driveway toward the Draeger home with a grin on his face and flutters in his stomach. Six months had gone by since he was here last, and in those six months, Adrian had had a lot to think about and plan. His beat-up truck was packed with everything he owned. Since the day his father had died, when he was in his teens, his only family had been the Draegers. His status as a member of the family was going to become official and permanent. Adrian was now a mated man, the same as married, and he couldn't wait to get started with his new life. The only drawback—he knew it was going to be an uphill battle.

Adrian's hair was medium brown, tending to turn blond in the summer months, hence he was often referred to as a golden shifter, and his eyes were baby blue. Most male shifters were dark in personality, but Adrian was different—carefree and lighthearted. Adrian stood at six-two. His hair was cut short at the back of his neck, but long on top. At times, the girls used to say he was a Brad Pitt look alike with an Orlando Bloom smile. His nose was straight and his lips full. He'd been told he was very kissable, and he had a body like a pro athlete. The only thing missing in his life was his mate, Skyler. The past six months without her had been torture for him.

Adrian smiled when he saw a brand new yard decoration in front of the house. The driveway he knew so well had changed, now a circle drive with a large water fountain in the middle and grass around it, with a very nice-looking arrangement of roses around the fountain. The one thing that came to mind was Sidney, Stefan's new wife, was making some major changes to the household. Adrian wondered how well Natasha, Stefan's mother, was taking it all. For years, that woman had single-handedly run this household, so Adrian wasn't so sure how it was going.

Jaden Sinclair

He stopped his truck on the left side of the fountain and put it into park, but he didn't get out. He sat back and gawked up at the house and thought about the last time he was here. Stefan had just gotten married, and Adrian had made a huge mistake that night, just before he went to talk to Stefan, and Dedrick—the head of the family—about placing his claim.

He knew that mistake was hanging over his head, and he began to have some doubt as to what he could do to fix it, thus making things right between him and Skyler. So far, he still had no clue how to make any changes. He hoped like hell Dedrick had Skyler at a point of understanding. After all, six months had gone by, plenty of time for her to cool off and work things out about him.

Sidney Draeger popped her head into the passenger side window with a bright smile on her face. "You do realize sitting out in the truck watching the house isn't going to work?"

It had been a long time since he had seen her, and he had to admit one thing, married life agreed with her. Her face was lit up like a Christmas tree, and the smile spread across her lips was one that could melt any man's heart. As far as Adrian was concerned, Stefan was one lucky bastard to have found a mate like Sidney. She was the perfect match for him, one who had Adrian dreaming and wishing. He wanted nothing more in his life than to get the same from Skyler.

"Well, you know…" Adrian smiled as he rested his right arm over the back of the truck seat and acted like he was thinking hard "…not quite sure what I'm about to get myself into once I go up those steps."

Sidney snorted, opened the door, and hopped inside. "I know what you mean. Let's run away."

"That bad?"

Sidney took a deep breath and brushed a few strands of her brown hair from her eyes. The rest was in a ponytail at the back of her head. Her hands were nearly as dirty as her jeans and blue T-shirt. Adrian clearly knew she had been digging in the dirt.

"Let's just say, I don't think I was quite that bad when Stefan brought me here." Adrian frowned at her, which got him a smile. "In the six months I've been here, I have never *ever* seen Skyler so pissed. What did you do?"

Adrian opened his mouth, but closed it. *How much to tell*, he thought. "Ah...um...well..." He cleared his throat. "Um..."

Sidney laughed. "That bad, huh."

Adrian took a deep breath. "It could be better." He let out a deep sigh mixed with a groan.

Sidney nodded and looked back at the house. "You know, Dedrick just told her this morning."

Adrian, his jaw dropping, turned his head to the right. "What?" he growled. "He was supposed to have that conversation six months ago."

She shrugged. "Well, he didn't."

"Son of a bitch," he moaned and dropped his head against the back of the seat.

Sidney patted his arm before opening the door. "Hope you have a cup back there," she smiled when he glanced at her. "She might go for your nuts."

"You're just Ms. Sunshine, aren't you?" He frowned as he slid from the truck, slamming his own door closed with extra force.

"Hey, when it comes to you guys," she said, walking around the truck to hook her arm through his and tug him to the front entrance, "I have zero sympathy."

Together, they walked up the stairs to the front door. Almost shoving Adrian inside, Sidney opened it, and when it closed, he started to feel like a cage was closing on him. He imagined the tension could be felt from everyone in the house. He stood in the foyer and peeked to the left to the huge dining room and then to the right where he knew the path led to Natasha's sitting room, which was also one of the ways to the family room in the back. When he saw no one, he finally glanced up the wide, wooden stairs in front of him. Up at the top, Stefan was leaning against the top railing with his arms crossed over his chest.

"Dedrick must still be in her room," Sidney told him while letting his arm go. "I'm going to wash up. "You," she pointed her finger at him, "stay put and deal with your mess."

Adrian growled.

"And don't growl at me," she said over her shoulder. "It doesn't work for Stefan, either."

Adrian shook his head and looked back up. Stefan was still focused on the closed door of Skyler's bedroom. Adrian felt something stir inside him. She was up there, so close all he had to do was run up there and take her. His woman. His!

"I know that look." Natasha strolled from the dining room without the friendly grin on her lovely face he knew so well. She was still a delicate-looking woman and the heart of the family. "Drake used to have it on his face when he became possessive. Drove me crazy." She walked up to him and took his face into her cool hands to bring him down to her height. Adrian was somewhat surprised when she kissed him on the cheek. "It's good to see you again, Adrian."

"Ms. Draeger," he acknowledged.

Natasha smiled and shoved him away gently. "No more of that crap." She patted him on the chest. "You will call me Natasha, young man, like I tell you every time you come here."

"Yes, ma'am." He grinned.

"Now." Natasha took a deep breath and, taking a step back from him, brushed at her blue slacks and silk top. A deep, serious expression furrowed her brow. "You want to explain all this to me?"

The look she gave him had Adrian feeling like he was a little boy once again. "I...um...I'm not really sure where to begin."

"How about—"

"Get out of my room!" Skyler Draeger screamed.

"Damn it, Skyler," Dedrick barked, clearly pissed off. "You're pushing it here."

"No, I'm standing my ground," she yelled. "I refuse to listen to you, him, or anyone for that matter."

On memory only, Adrian knew she had green eyes, and he would place all his money on the suspicion that right now, they were sparkling like emeralds with her anger. He couldn't stop the desire raging inside him.

"It doesn't work that way, Skyler." Adrian knew Dedrick was on the edge from the updates Stefan had given him. He just didn't think it had gotten to this point. "You know the rules. He has the right to make this claim."

"You have the right to refuse him," she screeched. "I don't want him or anyone else!"

"Well, too damn bad," Dedrick shot back. "I accepted it."

"You can't!" she growled out.

"As the head of the family, I can," he told her.

"Yeah, it's going well," Adrian remarked quietly.

"He should have prepared her earlier," Natasha said, crossing her arms over her chest. "I don't like how he's handling things. Dedrick's angry a lot and on edge."

"You need to get off your goddamn high horse and get that ass of yours downstairs to greet your mate properly," Dedrick barked, sounding dangerous to Adrian's ears.

"He isn't my mate!" She sounded just as pissed off as her brother. "What I should do is kick him in the balls for what he did to me."

Adrian moved to the stairs and stopped when he heard Dedrick yell, "He didn't do anything to you, yet, so don't try to pull any bullshit on me, young lady."

"Don't you 'young lady' me!" she yelled. "You are not my father."

"Excuse me, Adrian," Natasha said, walking past him to the stairs. "I think it's time I go up there and calm things down. See you at dinner."

Adrian knew Dedrick was beyond pissed off. Adrian had never heard him in a rage like this in all the years he had spent in the house growing up. Natasha stopped to speak to Stefan, who peered down at Adrian with a brief grin.

Stefan rushed down the stairs. "Man, it's about time you showed up." Stefan extended his arm, shaking Adrian's hand with a smile. "Was starting to think you were going to stay down there and hide."

"I see Dedrick waited until the last moment to tell her," Adrian said.

"Oh, you know Dedrick." Stefan took a deep breath, letting it out slowly. "Waits until the last second to deliver news he knows isn't going to be taken well." Stefan looked up the stairs. Natasha had disappeared into Skyler's room. "Come on. Let's go into the office and wait for the bear to come."

"Sounds like a plan to me."

Not even ten minutes went by before Dedrick barged into the office and slammed the door closed. "I knew this was going to give me another headache." Dedrick groaned.

"I'm sorry about this, Dedrick," Adrian said, feeling some guilt about how he had placed everything on the other man's shoulders. "Guess I handled this all wrong."

"No, doing it at a Gathering would have been wrong," Stefan said. He chuckled but quickly stopped when Dedrick gave him a dirty look.

"Well this is going to be very interesting." Dedrick rubbed his eyes and slumped into his chair behind the desk. "Who the hell told Mom?"

"Dedrick, come on." Stefan extended his arms. "It's Mom. She finds out everything."

"So what's the game plan now?" Adrian sighed.

Dedrick took many deep breaths while rubbing his temple as if he had a headache. "I have no idea. I told you this wasn't going to be easy, that she'd fight it all the way." He pointed his finger at Adrian and gave him a hard stare. "You're all on your own."

"Would have helped some to have told her before now," Adrian mumbled under his breath. When he peeked up at Dedrick, he saw his dark expression. "Come on," he cried. "You kind of left me here to walk into the lion's den alone."

Dedrick groaned, but it sounded more like a growl. "Why do you two dipshits always put this crap on my shoulders? Look, I told her. You didn't state when, only that I had to. I've done my part, be happy with that."

"Well, like you said, big brother." Stefan smiled, looking Dedrick in the eye. "You're the head of the house."

"I have half a mind to beat you to a bloody pulp," Dedrick said in a deadly voice. "Wipe that damn smile off your face." Stefan jumped back when Dedrick stood, pointing a finger at him, which caused Stefan to quickly lose the smile. "You are just damn lucky I don't kick your ass just for spite, but knowing your wife, she would get that friend of hers on *my* ass." He shook his head.

"Come on, Dedrick." Stefan sighed. "Jaclyn has only been around twice since the wedding, and I never saw her stalking you. Drooling maybe, but not stalking."

"Piss off, Stefan. And you." He pointed to Adrian. "You...you...well, you just...oh fuck! I give up."

Adrian shook his head when he saw Stefan chuckle at Dedrick as he walked away. Even Adrian knew he was on thin ice with Dedrick, and to laugh or push him further would be like taking his own life in his hands.

"You know, I'm starting to think he doesn't like me after all," Adrian remarked. "I think you have a death wish, too."

"Oh, I wouldn't worry so much about him." Stefan grinned. "It's your own nuts you should worry about. Skyler's out for your blood, my man. I have never seen her so pissed off before. What did you do?"

"Got me. Not a thing—yet." Adrian replied.

"He has no right to do this to me." Once again, Adrian heard Skyler yelling. This time, the sound was closer, like she had just rushed past the door.

"Here we go again." Stefan rolled his eyes.

* * * *

Adrian heard the stomping and quickly rose. He walked past a joyous-looking Stefan as he rushed out of the office and almost into Skyler. She stopped short and backed away from him as if he were some horrible creature.

Adrian cocked his head to one side, the corner of his lip going up. "Why?"

Skyler gaped at Adrian like he had lost his mind. "What?"

"I asked you why," he said, crossing his arms over his chest. "Why do you think I don't have the right to do this?"

"You have a lot of nerve showing up here," she growled, pointing her finger at him but not making a move to come any closer. "After what you did."

"After what I've done?" Adrian tried like hell to keep a straight face. He knew if he smiled, her rage would boil over to a new and more dangerous level, and he really didn't want to have it out with her about what he had done with her entire family standing around watching. So, instead of making more of a scene, Adrian took two steps closer to her so only she would hear what he had to say. "Would you have preferred it was you that night?"

The question seemed to be all it took for her to snap. Skyler's face turned about two shades brighter red, but Adrian couldn't tell if it was embarrassment or anger. She lunged at him, and Adrian was ready. He bent over, quickly picked her up, and slung her over his shoulder. Skyler screamed and started to kick and hit at him with all her might.

Adrian didn't look at Natasha and Dedrick, when he walked past them and toward the stairs with Skyler on his shoulder. He took the steps two at a time. He ignored the insults and dirty names Skyler flung at him as they went. He even managed to push away the urge to pop her one on her tight little ass that wiggled in the air with each step. Clearly, Skyler needed to understand a few things. She needed to listen to him, let him explain himself. Somehow, there had to be a way to get her to listen. In all the years he had known Skyler, Adrian had never seen her so pissed off. Yes, he did deserve her anger and hate, but he couldn't allow her to dish out the problem lingering between them in front of everyone. Adrian didn't need her family to find out what was going on, not yet, not until he knew how he was going to make it up to her.

Being the baby in the family and without a father, Skyler got away with just about everything. If she wanted something, both Stefan and Dedrick gave it to her, and if a boyfriend hurt her, they would always want to go out and hurt him. Natasha was always there to help mend Skyler's broken heart. So, when Adrian discovered his best friend's little sister had a crush on him, he had stayed the hell away. He knew how Skyler got when she wanted something, and he didn't want his friendship with Stefan broken up over her broken heart.

At the time, he couldn't and wouldn't give her what she wanted or what she thought she needed. If he had known then she would end up his mate, he would never have done what he had or put a claim on her the way he had. Sure, he knew all of this was going to be hard—coming back after six months to finish his claim, seeing the hurt and pain in her eyes when she looked at him, killed him, but he hadn't imagined it was going to be quite this hard or that she was going to have murder in her eyes.

Yet, at the same time, he couldn't risk having another male mark her. Once a mark was made on a female's shoulder that was it or was supposed to be it. Few males in their right mind, if they valued their lives, would pursue a marked female. Adrian was dying to mark Skyler, to show every male around that she was his.

Adrian walked to her bedroom, opened the door, and then kicked it closed. Skyler's bedroom was very large, and, to Adrian, very girly. She had a queen-size bed with a soft pink and white lace comforter. Nightstands were on each side of the bed. Next to the door on his left was a large dresser and at the foot of the bed, a vanity table and chair. She also had two window seats, her own bathroom, and a walk-in closet, which was open.

He walked up to the bed and tossed Skyler none too gently onto it. He grinned when she bounced and glared up at him. Adrian looked down at her, and he felt as if his heart landed in his throat. She was beautiful. Built just like her mother, Skyler had delicate hands and perfect hips that smoothed out to long legs he was dying to feel wrapped around his waist. Just gazing at her from his current angle, Adrian could tell her breasts were full and would fit into his hands as if molded for them alone. Her long dishwater-blonde hair tumbled carelessly down her back and swayed gently to her every movement with thin bangs on her forehead.

"You're an ass," she said, moving to the other side of the mattress away from him.

"No, I'm determined," he told her with his finger raised in the air. "There's a difference."

"Where you're concerned," she snapped, "I doubt it."

Adrian couldn't help himself and laughed. "You really think acting like this is going to make me just pack up my shit and leave? Boy, you're more deluded than I first thought."

"Well, what gave that away, Einstein?" she smarted back.

"So, what pisses you off the most?" Adrian dropped down on the mattress, lounging back at the foot of the bed on his side with a smile. "The claiming or the sex in the woods?"

"Adrian, get off my bed and get the fuck out of my room!"

"Tsk, tsk, tsk." He shook his head. "Such language from a lady."

Skyler scooted from the bed, walked to the door, and yanked it open. "Get out, Adrian."

Adrian closed his eyes and inhaled the sweet scent swirling around the room. It had been a long time since he had taken Skyler's scent into his lungs and let her essence fill him. For the long months he had been away, all he could do was think about her, dream about her, and crave her. He wondered if her skin was as soft as it looked, if she would feel like heaven once his arms wrapped around her.

Okay, looking at her now in her anger, she didn't seem all warm and fuzzy, but that didn't stop the desire or his dominant side from suffering. Control—that was what he needed at the moment. If he didn't pull it together, right now, he was going to make even more of an ass out of himself than he already had. With her glaring at him from the door of her bedroom, he found some of his control slipping.

She was so pissed off right now it caused her scent to become stronger, shooting right down to his cock, and as usual, the damn thing had a mind of its own. It came to life behind his jeans, thick and heavy, crying out for a claim, for freedom and pleasure. Adrian pictured Skyler laid out on the bed, spread, with arms out inviting him. The image had Adrian biting his lower lip to suppress a moan and the sudden throbbing that had formed between his legs. *Shit, my dick is what got me into trouble in the first place.*

"Adrian, I mean it," Skyler said. "Get out of my room!"

"I don't want to," he told her matter-of-factly. He stood up from the bed and walked to her.

"What are you doing?" she asked, uncertainty in her voice.

"What do you think I'm doing?" he asked, leaning against the door.

"I think you're being an ass," Skyler snapped at him and made a move to brush past him and out of the bedroom. Adrian grabbed her, and in one fluid motion, she turned on him and hit him with her fist. "You son of a bitch! What gives you the fucking right to lay claim on me? Go back to your goddamn whores and leave me the hell alone."

Skyler's nostrils flared in her anger as she jerked her arm from his hold to cross them over her chest. She lifted her head to glare up at him.

"I don't have whores, Skyler," Adrian, defeated, informed her. He rubbed his jaw where she'd hit him. "Nice punch."

"Oh, so you just fuck anyone then!" She snorted and jammed her hands on her narrow hips. "I understand now."

Adrian felt his patience slipping. He narrowed his eyes, watching her walk away from him, acting as if she were better than he was. It was a Skyler he never saw, not even years ago when she didn't get her way. She had never had this high-and-mighty attitude, but this wasn't a little girl any longer. This was a woman scorned. "And just what do you think you understand?" He slammed the door closed and enjoyed for a brief moment the way she jumped at the noise before he leaned against it.

"I understand you will fuck anyone who will spread their legs for you!" She turned, smiling all sweet and nice at him, but her eyes told him she was anything but sweet and nice at the moment. In fact, her expression told him that winning her forgiveness wasn't going to be easy like he had hoped it would be. "Then, when you want a mate, you go looking for the nice girls. I'm not your nice girl."

"You're being a bit childish," he told her. "For your information, I don't go out fucking every girl who opens for me. If I did, I would have done your girlfriend, years ago—in your bed." He smirked.

Skyler charged at him. "Go to hell, Adrian!" She made to hit him in the gut, but Adrian was ready for it.

He took the punch, pushed himself off the door, and walked toward her, forcing Skyler to back away. "Do you really think if I knew the outcome of all this, I would have done what I did?" Backing her up against a wall, he placed his hands next to her head, boxing her in. "Do you for one moment think I'd intentionally cause you pain or hurt you?" Anger vibrated in his voice.

"Yes, I do," she answered, with not one ounce of fear visible. She held her head high, almost daring him to do something.

Adrian raised one of his eyebrows. "Okay, I'll admit I fucked up royally." Feeling mischievous, he grinned. "If you'll admit you've had a crush on me all these years."

Her face paled. "Wh—wh…are you out of your damned mind?" she screeched, pushing against his chest. "I've never had a crush on you." Skyler flailed her arms. "I don't even like you, so why the hell would you think I had a crush on you?"

"Do you want me to prove it to you then?" Adrian worked damn hard at keeping his tone level and his body under control when all he felt was a raging need to claim. It was in a shifter's nature, once a claim was known, to take what was his. For Adrian to stand there with his mate and not touch or take what was rightfully his was damned difficult.

"There's nothing to prove," Skyler whispered.

He saw her swallow hard, could smell the nervousness in her. "Really?" He cocked his head to one side and grinned down at her. Adrian leaned into her, bringing his face as close to hers as he could without touching her. "Let's find out, shall we?" Quickly, he claimed her lips in a heated kiss. He moved one hand from the wall and cupped her ass.

Adrian brought Skyler nearer, and he deepened the kiss, forcing her to take his tongue. He moaned into her mouth while her arms went around his neck. He wasn't sure she realized she'd drawn him closer, but he took advantage of it. Adrian picked her up, wrapped her legs around his waist, and pushed her back against the wall. He groaned at the sweet, tortuous pleasure he felt.

Grinding into her, he kneaded her ass. He kissed her so deeply, he thought he might drown in the pleasure. The strongest thought at the moment was of stripping her bare, kissing her entire body, and leaving not one inch untouched. The thought was so strong it had his cock raging hard and painfully heavy in his jeans.

He wanted to feel her skin against his own, felt like he needed it and wouldn't be able to breathe without it. "God, you feel so good," he whispered against her lips just before he sucked her lower lip into his mouth. "This is meant to be, Skyler. Don't you know that? Can't you feel it?" He kissed her again, plunging his tongue into her mouth to mate with her own.

Skyler broke the kiss and pushed Adrian back. "No. I can't do this."

Adrian had his hands on her ass while she tried to push away from him. He relented and allowed her feet to fall back to the ground. "Skyler—"

"No!" Skyler pulled his hands from her ass, turned her back to him, and walked back to the door. "I can't trust you, Adrian, not after what you've done."

Adrian didn't say anything. He let her go, for now, and rested his forehead on the wall to get his body under control. "Fuck," he groaned, as he adjusted his hard cock. "This is not going to be easy at all."

* * * *

Skyler stood at the window overlooking the huge backyard. She was watching not only the cookout that was going on, but also the pool basketball game. Stefan and Adrian were in the pool, Sidney lounged in a chair next to the pool, and Dedrick cooked burgers on the grill.

Everyone was having a good time but her.

"You know, you can come down and enjoy dinner with us," Natasha said from the doorway of Skyler's room. "It would be the polite thing to do since we have a new member in our home."

"He's not a new member." Skyler snorted, crossing her arms over her chest, keeping her eyes on the game below. "He's nothing more than an intruder. He doesn't belong here."

Skyler could feel her mother's eyes on her, and it unnerved her. In all her years, she'd never known her mother to take someone else's side, and having her take Adrian's side was heartbreaking. Hell, what *Adrian* did was tearing her apart inside. Of all the things he could have done, putting a claim on her mere seconds after she caught him in the arms of another woman was unforgivable. What she saw the night of her brother's wedding would stay with her forever, just like her broken heart would always stay broken where Adrian was concerned. In her mind, she couldn't forgive him or trust him. Then again, he'd made it very clear a long time ago that he only cared for her as a sister. It had taken a very long time for Skyler to heal, and she thought she was over the hurt and had moved on. Given the way she was feeling at that moment, she wasn't as over it as she had thought.

Sweet sixteen was supposed to be the time of her life. Instead, she had spent it crying in her pillow. She had hoped that on her birthday she would get a kiss from the one she thought she loved, yet all she got was rejection. Adrian didn't want her. His friendship with her brother had meant more to him.

"Honey, I'm sure whatever it is you think he's done it isn't as bad as what you're making it out to be." Natasha placed her hands on Skyler's shoulders before pulling her back into her arms. Being held this way reminded Skyler of just how vulnerable she really was. "You should really work this thing out. He isn't going to go anywhere."

"You should make him go." Skyler shrugged off her mother's arms and turned from the window. "I'm going to fix a sandwich."

"Why don't you just come down and have dinner with us?" Natasha sighed.

"Because right now, I can't stand the sight of Adrian Laswell."

She walked past her mother with her head lowered so she wouldn't be able to see the untruth of her words. She didn't hate the sight of Adrian. She still loved looking at him, even though it brought her pain, and she quickly made her way out of the room, leaving her mother there alone. Skyler shook her head. She didn't understand how a man could go from wanting nothing to do with her to suddenly placing a claim.

She headed down to the kitchen sure she would be alone since it seemed everyone was outside. The kitchen, like the rest of the house, was big. Dark oak cabinets lined the walls in a U-shape with an island in the middle. Natasha Draeger had skimped on nothing with the building of the house after the original burned down before Skyler was born. Skyler headed straight for the stainless steel refrigerator to make herself a sandwich. She didn't even look up or stop her search when she heard the back door open.

"Steak or hamburger?" A plate was lowered over the refrigerator door and in front of her face, but Skyler didn't need to glance up to know who held the plate. Once a girl got her first taste of what Adrian sounded like, she never forgot.

"Neither," she answered coldly. Skyler straightened and looked at him with contempt. When her eyes traveled lower to the green towel wrapped around his waist, she felt as if she had been hit with a longing she had thought was long forgotten. "Suddenly, I've lost my appetite."

He sighed, tossing the plate on the island when she closed the door and turned away from him. "Skyler," Adrian called out and then sighed again loudly. "How long do I get to expect this?"

Skyler turned on her heels a few inches away from him. "Expect what?"

One hand went to his hip, the other rubbed at his jaw before he took one step closer to her. The hand that had rubbed his jaw made a motion around the room. "This, us, the attitude you seem to have screaming you're so much better than me."

"I never thought I was better than you," she whispered, frowning at him.

"Well, you sure as hell could have fooled me." He snorted and rubbed his face in an irritated manner. "Come on, Skyler." He sighed. "This fighting isn't going to solve anything or make it go away like you want. We need to talk about it."

Claiming Skyler

"Oh, and I don't care for the way you put a claim on me after you did what you did," she barked at him. "I have a life, Adrian, and it doesn't involve you." Stepping closer to him, she jabbed her finger in his chest. "Did you even stop to think that I might have a boyfriend or another guy I'm thinking about mating with, or did you just not give a damn?"

"If you're talking about Thomas Fallen, I know all about him," he told her with such calm that she wanted to rip out his hair and scratch his eyes out. "He isn't the kind of guy that can handle you."

"Handle! Handle, me!" she screeched, seeing red. "No one handles me."

Amusement crossed his face. "I think I am starting to see that."

"Argh!" Skyler charged him and realized it was a mistake. When she swung at him, Adrian grabbed a hold of her, picked her up, and set her down on the island with him standing between her legs, holding her wrists behind her back.

"Where did you get that temper?" he asked her sweetly. "And while we're on the subject, who taught you how to hit like that?"

"None of your damn business." She struggled against him until she got her hands free to push at his chest, kicking her legs. "Now get your fucking hands off me."

"You know I'm going to get what I want." Adrian's voice thickened, and his blue eyes darkened in what Skyler suspected was desire. "If I have to play dirty, Skyler, I will. I'll do anything I have to do in order to have you."

"In your dreams," she taunted, grinning at him. "I'm not yours to have, Adrian. Get used to it." She tried to push against him, but it was like pushing a brick wall.

Adrian smiled, showing his even white teeth. "Oh, baby, if you knew what I dreamed about, you would be blushing for weeks." He moved her hands so he could hold them with one of his. With his free hand, he took hold of her chin and forced her to look at him.

Skyler stared into the blue of his eyes and slowly started to feel herself drawn in. Her mouth went dry, palms turned sweaty.

"Fuck it," he whispered. Adrian kissed her. His hands left her wrists to cup her head, and he kissed her deeply. Slowly, she felt as if she was falling into the kiss, drowning in sensations she had never experienced. She was so lost that she didn't know when her eyes closed, but she felt as if she couldn't open them.

She couldn't speak when his lips left hers to trail down her jaw to her left shoulder. Adrian kept kissing her neck as he pulled her shirt over, exposing her shoulder.

"You're mine, Skyler," he murmured against her shoulder. He licked and sucked at the flesh. "You just have no clue what I'll do to have you." His teeth scraped her shoulder in the same spot that would one day hold the mark of her mate. "So keep one thing in mind. All bets are off." His voice rumbled in what she took as a warning growl. "Let the games begin."

Biting her gently, he sucked hard on her shoulder. Skyler moaned at the light pain, and then her eyes snapped open when it went through her system to pool between her legs in an intense throbbing need.

Laughter by the back door broke them apart. Adrian let go of her shoulders to look up in the direction of the door. Skyler felt as if she was ready to strip and let him have whatever he wanted.

"There's more beer in the fridge," Stefan called.

Hearing her brother's voice was like ice water to her face. Skyler pushed Adrian away from her as hard as she could. She glared, straightened her shirt, and hopped down from the counter. When the door opened and Stefan walked in, Skyler slapped Adrian across the face hard, leaving a red mark across his cheek. "I'm not playing games," she said in a tight voice. "Stay the hell away from me!"

* * * *

They were entwined on her bed, legs rubbing against legs. Skyler felt the passion rise in her body just as she felt his desire for her in the stiffness of his cock pressing against her stomach. Adrian's hands roamed over her body with his hot lips following. She was on fire for him, and it seemed the temperature only increased with each caress.

He moved between her legs, his stiff cock pressing against the core of her sex. They danced in an erotic tale of passion, his kiss molten on her neck, and his hands were teasing and tender when they brushed her breasts.

Claiming Skyler

"No one else is going to make you feel like this," he told her smoothly. He spoke directly in her ear. "No other will ever touch you, but me."

Skyler sat up in bed with a start. She was breathing hard. Sweat beaded her forehead, face, and even the tank-top she slept in was wet. She knew how Stefan had seduced Sidney with his mind, but not in her wildest dreams or nightmares did she think Adrian was capable of doing the same thing to her.

"You shit," she grumbled, wiping her face. Skyler frowned when she heard a faint laughing in her head. "I'll get you for this," she mumbled under her breath, turning over in her bed and beating the pillow. "Oh, I will get even with you."

Chapter Two

Sleep evaded her most of the night. Skyler sat on the side of her bed thinking about the past and what Adrian had just done to her. It was hard for her to trust him, hard to look at him knowing what he had done. It wasn't so much about the claim. Hell, if she'd never seen him in the woods with another woman, she would have been happy to know he had put a claim on her, but she'd seen him. Now she was as far from happy as she could get. In her eyes, he was doing just like all the rest of the hot shots out there—mess around with the bad girls, and then when he wanted a respectable mate, he came to a proper girl. Well, it wasn't going to work this time, not for Adrian. She'd be damned if she was going to make any of this easy for him. There was no way in hell she was going to forgive him for this.

If she was so sure, why did it hurt like hell? *Because, you fool, you don't have a crush on him. You're in love with him.* Skyler dropped her face into her hands and tried to stop the tears from spilling. She shook her head, fighting the truth even though deep in her heart, she knew it was right. Somewhere along the way, a very long time ago, she had stopped having a crush and had fallen in love with him.

"Hey, I need to go shopping for a few things and wondered if you might want to go?" Sidney walked into Skyler's bedroom digging into the huge bag that Sidney insisted was her purse. Stefan teased her all the time about carrying a suitcase instead of a purse. "Jacy's coming for a few days and—" She stopped and glanced up at Skyler.

Skyler knew that her face was pale. She saw it after she got out of the shower at two in the morning. After what Adrian had pulled on her, there was no way in hell she was going to get back to sleep, not that she was going to try.

"You look as if you haven't slept."

"I didn't," Skyler told her while standing up and hugging her robe closer. "At all," she added under her breath. She walked into her closet, grabbed some clothes and came back out only to go into the bathroom to get dressed. When she came out, she was dressed in jeans and a short T-shirt that showed off her belly. "So why is Jaclyn coming?"

"Oh, she just got back from wherever. I'm trying to get her to settle down some and stay put. Thought I might guilt her into staying here, maybe moving in." Sidney walked over to the bed, tossed her bag on it, and then plopped herself down on the side. "There is definitely enough room. If only I could get her to stay put. She claims she is a free spirit and needs to be on the go all the time. I call it on the run, and I have a pretty good idea what she's running from."

"Mom's okay with this?" Skyler sat down at her vanity table and began to brush her long hair before pulling it back into a tail.

"Why would I have to check it out with Natasha?" Sidney asked. "I thought this was my home, too."

Skyler stopped what she was doing and turned around in her seat to face Sidney. "It is." She sighed before turning back to finish with her hair and the light makeup she wore. "I just have a lot on my mind." She shrugged. "Don't pay attention to me."

Silence hung in the room, and it was a while before Sidney spoke again. "Skyler, what's really going on?"

Skyler finished pulling her hair into a ponytail but didn't turn around. She thought about what was going on, and everything that came to mind had to do with Adrian. He used to come around in the summers a lot, almost becoming another member of the family. Adrian's father also came around to help Stefan and Dedrick out with hunting, with how to be men, with what the signs were when their mates were close, and dealing with their heat. But after the death of his father, Adrian had changed. He had been forced to grow up, but Skyler knew he hadn't grown up as much as he should have.

Skyler had been nineteen almost twenty before she finally gave up on the idea of ever being with Adrian. He was just out of her range, and he hadn't seemed to notice her as a young woman who could make him a great mate. He had seen her as a little sister and that had hurt. Back then, she'd wanted him to see her as a woman, not a little girl, but he hadn't.

Sure, he had flirted with her, but she had felt like he only did that to be nice to her since Stefan always picked on her.

What had happened six months ago at Stefan's wedding had confirmed that she and Adrian just weren't meant to be. Seeing him with another girl in his arms had crushed her dream to a point that she had to move on. So, using the time he had stayed away to mend what was left of her heart, Skyler got on with her life and had finally started to date Thomas Fallen behind her brothers' backs. And then, lo and behold, Adrian drifted back into her life only to rip it apart once again. How was she going to tell her boyfriend that another man had put his claim on her months ago, and she'd had no idea about it?

"It's nothing, Sidney," she finally answered. "Just have a lot on my mind, is all."

"The best way to get things off your mind I've found," Sidney said with a smile, "is to go out and spend money."

Skyler looked at her and found it impossible not to smile. Sidney's eyes were shining, and there was a certain glow about her.

"I have the credit card," Sidney sang.

Skyler chuckled. "Okay. Since my brother is paying, I'm getting that dress I've been eyeing for the annual party."

Standing up, Sidney lugged her bag over her shoulder. "Yeah, your brother was telling me your mother puts on this huge party every year." She frowned at Skyler. "Why?"

"It's our new year party," Skyler told her. "It's when a lot of the families come together to celebrate births and the adulthood of shifter children. Oh, and new marriages." She grinned and followed Sidney out of her room. "Kind of like the parties your kind has. What are they called? New Year's Eve."

"But it doesn't happen until next year," Sidney said, peeking over her shoulder. "So why is Natasha doing all of this now?"

"Because she usually invites more people than what the house can handle." Skyler laughed. "Mom loves to have parties. We used to have them all the time when we were little. She'll open up the back wing of the house and hire a staff for a short time, that kind of thing." Skyler shrugged.

"Maybe I can use that as the excuse to keep Jaclyn here longer, which in turn I can use to talk her into moving in."

Sidney dug into her bag once again while she talked, and Skyler shook her head. Stefan was right; the girl needed a better and smaller purse.

"Ah, there they are," Sidney said. She pulled out her keys. "I got the car also."

Skyler laughed. "You're the only one I know who has not only gotten Stefan to give that card of his over, but the keys to his car as well. How'd you do it?"

"I have my ways, girlfriend." With a wicked grin, Sidney draped her arm over Skyler's shoulders. "Now, let's go and seriously spend some money."

* * * *

"Adrian, can I speak with you?" Natasha asked when Adrian came down the stairs.

She was in her sitting room, and Adrian felt like he was a little boy again and in major trouble. Natasha never called out to speak with one of them in the cool tone she was using at that moment unless she was slightly pissed off at them. Adrian had wondered how long it was going to take before she wanted to have a talk with him.

"Sure," he answered and took a deep breath, steeling himself for the worst.

"Please." Natasha smiled. "You act like you're about to step into a dungeon."

"Well, you do have the same look in your eyes, if my memory serves me right, from that time Stefan broke your vase." He grinned and sat down in the wingback chair across from her.

Natasha snorted. "I know it was you and not him. You two were playing ball in the house, and you were up to bat." She sat back in her chair, arms folded over her chest, and one leg crossed over the other. "He took your spanking."

"I know." He chuckled. "I had to give him my best baseball card for it, but it was worth it." He smiled.

Natasha smiled in such a lady-like manner that Adrian forgot he was here for what he suspected was his lecture. Stefan's mother was one of a kind in his eyes, so gentle and soft, but could be a true hard-ass if the occasion called for it. On more than one occasion, he wondered what Drake Draeger had been like—wondered how he'd held onto this strong-willed woman.

"Adrian, I don't want you to hurt Skyler," Natasha finally said, her blue eyes grabbing his full attention. "I don't know what has happened between the two of you, and I really don't want to know. What I do want is for my history to not repeat itself on my daughter."

"Natasha, if that were the case, I would have carried her out the front door six months ago," Adrian informed her dryly. He didn't like the way this conversation was going and had to keep reminding himself to show respect for his mate's mother, like he always had, but inside, an animal was screaming for control, screaming to claim. Adrian couldn't stand Natasha's cold stare or the anger in those eyes any longer, and he stood and strolled to the window. Looking out at the lawn, he tamped down his own frustration over this situation. "I didn't plan for this, and believe me when I say that if I knew what was going to happen, I would have done things a whole lot differently."

Natasha made a very unladylike sound that had Adrian turning back around to her. "The signs were always there. You were just too busy playing the stud game to notice." Adrian opened his mouth to speak, but was cut off. "Skyler let go of you for reasons I don't know. Adrian, she has been dating someone, and he doesn't know about any of this."

"I know about Thomas." He said the name as if it had a very bitter taste. As much as he tried, Adrian couldn't get it out of his head that Skyler had indeed begun dating another man after he had made his claim on her. "I'm prepared to take care of it."

"That's not your place," Natasha said in the authoritative air that he knew meant business when she was speaking to her family. "Skyler has to do it." She stood up without her usual tender smile. "I know this is hard for you, and I know that time is something you men don't like to give, but she needs it. We have at least a week and half until the full moon, with a few days less for her cycle, so I'm putting it on your shoulders here. Don't press too hard, Adrian. If you do, she will resent you for the rest of your lives. Skyler doesn't have too much room left in her heart when it comes to you. I would hate for what's left to be torn apart."

* * * *

Dinner that night was very tense with the whole family seated around the dining room table. Natasha fixed a huge supper but with so many shifter males around the table, it had to be. All shifter men ate like there was no tomorrow.

When Sidney came back from her shopping trip, loaded with bags, Adrian heard something he hadn't heard in a very long time—Skyler laughing. She came in the front door with Sidney, laughing and joking like the girl he remembered. Almost as soon as it had it started, it stopped when she saw him, and it hurt like hell. He wanted her to smile and laugh with him, not try to run because of him. Now she sat across from him at the table, doing everything she could not to look at him or talk to him.

"Adrian." Natasha pulled him out of his thoughts to hand him the bowl of potatoes.

He glanced down, spooning some onto his plate before handing it over to Sidney. Another bowl followed until he had everything on his plate, and then, once again, his eyes and thoughts went back to Skyler. He saw the stiffness in her jaw, the way she worked at avoiding his eyes. If he didn't know better, he would think that something was about to blow, and he prayed like hell that it happened after dinner. What he dreaded the most was the whole family finding out what he had done. He wanted to keep it between him and Skyler, but his gut was screaming that it wasn't to be.

Sidney broke the silence in the room. "So, tell me about this party."

Adrian had his eyes fixed on Skyler. He picked up on the fact that everyone at the table was acting strange, almost like a storm was brewing, one he was sure was going to begin to rage right here tonight.

"Well," Natasha began, "the whole backyard ends up being full of guests. Some will stay overnight. I usually have food brought in and set up outside, and we have a dance floor, too."

"Sounds like a ball." Sidney giggled.

"Natasha is famous for her parties," Adrian said, turning to Sidney and flashing her a quick smile before taking a bite out of his chicken leg.

"Adrian is famous for enjoying them," Skyler put in out of the blue, getting all eyes at the table focused on her.

"Skyler," Natasha warned.

Adrian put the chicken leg down on his plate, wiped his mouth with the napkin, and sat back in his chair to wait for her to let the cat out of the bag. He had no doubt she was about to tell her whole family what he had done. He had hoped to discuss this with her alone. What he did was bad enough, but to have her tell everyone at the dinner table would be brutal.

"Remind me again," Skyler went on, keeping her voice level, sounding sweet. "What is it you like to do at parties?"

"Skyler," Natasha tried again. "I really think—"

"Oh, now I know..." She smiled, and then laughed.

Adrian felt his heart drop when she finally looked at him. He didn't see anger, but pain. Skyler was still hurting over it all, and it was killing him. He sat forward in his chair, staring at her dead on. "If you want to talk about this, let's go in the other room."

"But why?" she asked him sweetly. "Don't you think my brothers have a right to know what kind of man they have allowed to put a damn claim on me?"

She finished with so much bitterness that he flinched. "What kind of man?" Frowning, he narrowed his eyes on her. "Why don't you stop and think about this for once. I could have demanded the claim at the Gathering and taken you away from your family." His anger was rising. "And if you want to bring your brothers into this, you better think carefully, sweetheart, because once you let it go, there's no taking it back."

"I think everyone needs to calm down," Natasha said.

Adrian had his full attention fixed on Skyler, and his heart was pounding. He wasn't afraid that she would tell. Hell, he knew it was going to come out eventually. Yet, at the same time, he needed to let her know that he wasn't going away just because she was pissed off and where he was concerned, she wasn't calling the shots. No matter how badly he wanted her, Skyler Draeger wasn't going to push him around in order to get what she wanted, which was out of this claiming. She could be pissed off at him until hell froze over, but he wasn't going to give her up. She was his heart. He just had to figure out a way to let her know it.

"Why don't you go back to doing what you do best?" Skyler tossed her napkin on the table and stood so quickly in her anger that her chair toppled over. "I'm sure there are many girls just lining up for you to take them out into the backyard. Or would you prefer to wait until there's another party before you take one of my friends into the woods and fuck her!"

The room stilled. Natasha sucked in her breath, Sidney dropped her fork, and Dedrick and Stefan stopped moving, one with a fork up to his mouth, the other with a cup in his hand. Adrian narrowed his eyes at Skyler, who was leaning on the table, breathing hard, tears in her eyes, but none falling.

Adrian stood slowly, placing his own napkin down on the table gently. "Let's cut the crap here, Skyler." He kept his voice even and his body calm. "You're not pissed off that I had sex with your friend, at your brother's wedding, or pissed off that I put a claim on you that night." He looked her dead in the eyes. "You're raging pissed because I didn't take *you* out there." His own voice rose in anger, and Adrian didn't give a damn that there was an audience watching this whole exchange. "So, why don't you fucking admit it and get it over with!"

"You're damn right I'm pissed," she cried, the first tear falling. "It should have been me!" she screamed before covering her mouth with her hand. "You bastard," she whispered before dropping her hand and lowering her eyes as more tears fell. "You fucking bastard." She turned her back on them and ran from the room.

"I'm going to be sick," Sidney suddenly said, reminding Adrian that there were still others in the room with them.

Sidney also ran from the room, and Adrian, feeling one weight lifted from his shoulders only to have another replace it, dropped back down in his chair.

"Adrian Joseph Laswell," Natasha said, her tone hushed but full of the authority that had always had them all cringing as boys and still as men.

Adrian turned to Stefan. "Did she have to use my middle name?"

"I want to know what the hell is going on in this house!" Natasha demanded, slamming her hand down on the table, which caused them all to jump. "I'm holding you," she pointed to Dedrick, "responsible for this."

"Me!" Dedrick cried, shock all over his face.

"Yes, you." Her pitch rose, letting all three know exactly how angry she was with them. "If you would have told her months ago, then it wouldn't have been this bad. And you." She glared at Adrian. "You had sex with one of her friends in *my* backyard?"

"Well…I…um…" Adrian stuttered.

"Save it," she yelled, causing them all to jump again. "I'm disappointed in all three of you."

"Three!" Stefan said, frowning at his mother. "What did I do?"

Natasha waved him off. "I don't care what you three idiots have to do, but I want this mess fixed." She shook her head. "I don't understand this. You three have me feeling like I'm the ring master at a circus. After what we went through when Stefan brought Sidney home, the threat of her father over our heads, and now this!" She sighed, looking both disappointed and hurt.

It tore at Adrian that he had caused this pain

"I know I raised you two to be better than this and to act reasonably." She pointed at Stefan and Dedrick. "And Adrian, I treated you like a son. I would expect the same from you as I do them." Adrian opened his mouth to defend himself, but Natasha silenced him with her hand. "No! No more tonight, please. I'm going to go up and check on my daughter." She turned her attention back to Dedrick. "This is your responsibility as head of this family!"

"This is his mess." Dedrick pointed at Adrian. "Not mine. I only did what he requested as the male placing his claim."

"Oh, this is just as much your mess as his, Dedrick Allen Draeger." That made Dedrick wince and Adrian smile. She pushed herself away from the table and tossed her napkin over her plate. "I knew I should have dealt with this on my own," Natasha mumbled, shaking her head and walking away.

"Well, that went well." Sighing, Stefan slumped back in his own chair.

Claiming Skyler

"Why the fuck didn't you tell me?" Dedrick demanded, glaring at Adrian. "I could have used the heads up."

Adrian stood back up, stacking dishes and keeping his eyes on the job. "I didn't think it was going to come out this way nor did I think it was anyone's business."

"You didn't think?" Dedrick also stood up, taking the dishes in hand. "That's the problem with you, Adrian. You don't fucking think!" he snapped. "And it *was* our mother-fucking business," he growled.

"Look, I wasn't expecting any of this to happen." Adrian tried to defend himself but knew that no matter what he said, he was in the doghouse with everyone. "How was I supposed to know that Skyler was going to blurt it out over dinner?" He went to the kitchen, placed the dishes in the sink, turned, and went back out for more with Dedrick following suit. Stefan was still sitting in the chair looking lost.

"You slept...no, let me correct that." Dedrick stopped, raised his hand in the air to stop Adrian from moving. "You had sex with her friend, in the backyard, at the wedding?"

"And Skyler caught me." Adrian sighed. "Happy now?"

"Oh no," Stefan groaned, covering his face with one hand.

"Then you dragged me into my own office to tell me you're going to claim her?" Dedrick's tone rose to a shout and a vein was throbbing in his neck, clearly showing how pissed Dedrick was at the moment, but Adrian didn't back down. "You claim my sister with another girl's scent still on you?"

Yep. Dedrick was pissed enough to kill, and it showed in the bright red color on his face. "What'd you want me to say, Dedrick?" Adrian asked. "Don't you think I know the mess I'm in?" Adrian suddenly felt tired, like all the fight was slowly leaving him. It felt like all he could do was stand there, and let whoever wanted to land the first punch. If he wasn't sorry for what he'd done before, he sure as hell was now.

"Oh, this is beyond a mess," Stefan said.

"Shut up!" Dedrick yelled at him with a growl. "I ought to kick your ass and toss it out of this house but that won't solve a fucking thing." Dedrick placed one hand on his lean hip, the other he dragged through his hair as he started to pace the dining room. "First Stefan drags his mate home, and now this," he mumbled.

"Dedrick…" Adrian started to say, but he stopped when Dedrick, not turning to face him, put his hand up. Adrian stared at Dedrick's rigid spine.

"Don't talk," Dedrick said. He walked around the room a couple more times before he stopped and glared at Adrian. "It's Tuesday. You have until Friday to finish your claim or I'm rebutting it."

"Wait one damn minute." Adrian got instantly pissed off. "I have my claim, goddamn it!"

"I'm giving you the rest of the week to finish it or it's over," Dedrick barked back, clearly mad as all hell. "You're a family friend, and that's the only thing keeping you in this position as it is. If you were Thomas and pulled this shit, I would have your ass." He finished with a deep growl.

"Fine." Adrian slammed the dishes back on the table, giving Dedrick his own angry look. "Your sister will be mine, completely, by the end of the week, but you get to handle Thomas. I want that prick gone and out of her life now!" Dedrick nodded his agreement. "And another thing," Adrian continued, glaring at the man before him. "I don't want any of your bullshit on how I do it, either. Friday, Skyler will hold my mark, willing or unwilling." Before Dedrick could argue with him further, Adrian turned and stormed out of the dining room.

* * * *

Pacing the bedroom that he had been given, Adrian kept glancing at the clock on the nightstand every three steps. It was only two after ten, and he wanted it to be midnight. Midnight was the best time to get into her mind.

Adrian had never used mind seduction on a girl before, at least nothing more than messing with them as they dreamed. He never had a reason to do so, until now, and with Dedrick giving him a deadline, he had to use everything he had to get Skyler.

He stopped again to look at the clock and groaned. Three after ten. Time was not going by fast enough for him.

Thomas Fallen crossed his mind while he paced once again. He remembered Thomas, or more accurately, his sister. Lorie Fallen had been Adrian's first lover, and boy, had she ridden him hard that night.

She'd just turned eighteen, had been chasing after him since they were sixteen. Thomas decided to throw his baby sister a party on her eighteenth birthday, and Adrian had been invited only because she pouted about it. Thomas didn't like Adrian, and he had good reason. Once Thomas had discovered the two of them in her bedroom, the dislike had turned to hate. Thomas had sworn to get even with Adrian for ruining his sister, never knowing that it had been Lorie who showed Adrian a thing or two. Lucky for Adrian, he didn't have a sister of his own because Thomas might have set out to destroy her. So, for Adrian, he had good reason not to trust Thomas or the little dating thing he was doing with Skyler.

"Argh." Feeling his beast rising, he pushed his hands into his hair. "Come on," he said through his teeth, glaring once more at the clock.

"Willing the time to move faster doesn't work."

Stefan grinned when Adrian whipped around. He was leaning against the door frame looking at Adrian like he knew just what he was doing.

"I can't believe your brother has backed me into this kind of corner," Adrian said, his hands landing on his waist. He knew he appeared a mess. "Your mother isn't going to like how this ends."

"Mom wants us to *not* follow in Dad's footsteps." Stefan took a deep breath, but his grin never left his lips. "We're supposed to be gentlemen when it comes to claiming our mates, not drag them home." He shrugged. "Just blame it on Dedrick."

"Stefan, this isn't funny," Adrian snapped. "Do you realize what I'm being forced to do? I have until Friday to put my mark on your sister."

Stefan rubbed his jaw before he spoke again. This time all humor was gone. "I understand, Adrian, really I do. I had to do almost the same thing with Sidney. Dedrick's just on edge lately, and with you keeping that from us, I guess it kind of hit him below the belt. Each month Mom and I have noticed that his heat is getting worse, so don't be surprised if he goes ahead and kicks your ass."

"And you?"

Stefan gave him a mischievous grin, moved closer, and, before Adrian could block it, landed his fist hard in his stomach. "I'm good now."

Adrian went to his knees. The air rushed out of his lungs and refused to come back in as he held his gut. Adrian forgot how sneaky Stefan could be, but the blow reminded him. Stefan could land a blow guaranteed to bring you down to your knees. "I…guess…I…deserved…that." Adrian struggled to speak.

"Well, I couldn't have you thinking that I didn't give a damn about my baby sister now, could I?" Stefan smiled. "Here, let me help you up, you big puss."

Adrian held out his hand for Stefan to stop trying to help him up. "I'm good," he gasped.

"Now, back to what I was saying." Stefan went on as if he hadn't just sucker punched his best friend. "Dedrick will come around in the end. He always does."

"And Skyler?" Coughing, Adrian struggled to get to his feet and staggered to the side of the bed.

Stefan took a deep breath and let it out slowly. "Skyler is hurt, man. Now we know why, but at the same time, I know that you're going to have to do what you feel is right. I can't tell you what to do, just like Mom or Dedrick can't. I've been in the same shoes as you, so I do know where you're coming from. I also know the stories from Mom on how males claimed in the old days. I don't want to see Skyler dragged from here and forced like that. I don't want a male coming into her life and demanding she lie down and accept her fate like they used to do it. Now, don't get me wrong, I don't like how Dedrick has forced the time here, and I do care about my sister, but if you want this claim to stand, you have to put your mark on her."

Stefan walked up to Adrian and put his hand on the other man's shoulder. "I trust you, man. No matter what mistakes you've made or what you do now, you are the man for my sister. If you weren't, she wouldn't have tried to get you a long time ago. But you hurt her again, and this time my foot is going to be the next thing for you to worry about."

He patted Adrian on the shoulder. "Now, do what you need to and finish this." Stefan turned and walked back to the door. He opened it and turned, eying Adrian from the doorway. "Oh, and she's already asleep, so you don't have to wait until midnight." He winked at Adrian before closing the door.

Adrian grinned, shaking his head. Of all the things one would expect a brother to say, having one tell him to seduce his baby sister wasn't it. The punch, yes. In fact, Adrian would have been slightly upset if Stefan hadn't done something like that. He turned once more at the clock and grinned, seeing it was ten to eleven. Stefan was right. He really didn't need to wait until midnight if she was already asleep. He reached behind his head, pulled his shirt up over his head, and tossed it aside. He worked his feet at removing his shoes while he unbuckled his belt, and then unbuttoned and unzipped his jeans. In only his tight boxer briefs, Adrian jumped onto the bed, smiling as he bounced into the middle. He became stone hard when he thought about what he was going to do. Another night of sweet mind seduction was at hand for his beloved Skyler.

Adrian rubbed his hands together before linking his fingers over his stomach. He took several deep breaths and let them out slowly to relax his body and mind. He closed his eyes and let his mind do its thing.

Adrian saw her lying on the bed, the blankets pushed down her legs to rest just below her knees. Her chest was covered by a top with spaghetti straps, and she wore matching panties that had thin strings on the sides. Adrian walked to the foot of the bed and looked down at her sleeping form. He knew this was a dream, and that he was in her mind, but at times like this, it was hard to separate the two.

Slowly, Adrian crawled onto the bed with a mere fraction of space between Skyler and him. As he held himself over her, he kissed the small amount of her belly showing. He moved slowly up to her breasts. He blew hot air over her breasts, which caused her nipples to get taut. Using his legs only, he spread hers to fit his hips as he lowered his body down to hers gently. Adrian felt his beast trying to claw its way out. Even in this dream state, he felt tortured having her under him at last.

Skyler had her eyes closed, but Adrian wished they were open and she was awake to really see and feel what he did. His hands roamed down the side of her body to the bottom of her top. Slowly, he pushed the fabric up, pulling it up over her breasts, allowing his heated mouth to close over one nipple. All Skyler did was squirm and wrap her legs and arms around him, bringing him closer. Adrian smiled. Skyler thought she was having a dream, and in a sense, she was. Adrian was giving Skyler the kind of dream that she needed to help push her right into his arms.

"God, you feel good," he whispered in her ear.

He moved his hands inside her panties to fondle her ass, squeezing the flesh and probing between her legs. "I could eat you alive," he told her, his voice thick with need. "And make love to you all night long."

When one of his hands moved to her wet pussy, Skyler's eyes opened, and shock was all over her face. "Adrian!" Her hands came up to his bare chest in a halfhearted attempt to push him away.

"Let me love you like it's meant to be," he whispered in her ear, brushing his lips across the lobe.

Adrian decided to send some hormones that were a lot like endorphins to Skyler in order to heat things up. When he had been with Lorie, he had discovered that he could do this, and it always made things interesting. It was a nice trick when he wanted to heat things up or help a girl out.

The moment those endorphins hit, Skyler moaned, and Adrian kissed her, sucking on her tongue as if it were candy. Right before he could slip a finger into her sweet heat, Skyler broke the spell, and he lost the connection.

Adrian lay on the bed, breathing hard. He looked at the clock, smiling when it finally struck midnight. His whole seduction had taken forty-five minutes, and now all he had to do was wait for Skyler to come and confront him. He didn't have long to wait.

Ten minutes later, Skyler barged into his room, slamming the door behind her. Nothing but a robe covered her luscious body. Adrian knew he was sporting a nice size erection at the moment and that it might scare her off, but he did *not* cover himself, and the expression on her face was priceless.

"Something wrong?" he asked innocently, working hard not to smile at her.

"Don't lie there acting as if you haven't done anything wrong," she yelled, shaking with anger as she walked over to the bed. "That was a really fucking lame thing to do."

Adrian moved his hand under his head and tried to keep an innocent expression on his face. "And just what did I do?" Not being able to handle it any longer, Adrian grinned.

Skyler began to hit him and scream, "You're a real asshole!"

Adrian couldn't stop laughing at her while he tried to fend off her blows. The more he laughed, the angrier Skyler seemed to get, which caused her to hit harder. When she took a step back from him, Adrian reached up quickly and took hold of her wrist. That move only fueled her anger more, and Skyler tried to slap at his face. Adrian ended up taking hold of both wrists and pulling her down to the bed, on top of him. When that didn't stop her, Adrian flipped her over onto her back and covered her with his body.

Adrian pinned Skyler to the bed and quickly positioning himself between her legs, letting her feel his stiff cock against her mound while he tortured himself even more. He glanced down at her breasts when her robe slightly parted.

"Mmm, very nice, Skyler," he murmured, licking his lips.

"Stop that, you perv," she cried out, trying to wiggle her wrists out of his hands. "Let me go!"

Holding her wrists with one hand, Adrian pulled them over her head. "No," he told her. With his other hand, he opened her robe for a better view.

Just viewing her body, having her so close, taking her sweet scent into his lungs, Adrian couldn't control himself. He had to touch her, had to feel the texture of her skin. He placed one hand flat against her stomach just under the top. With a slowness that would allow him to savor each and every feeling, he moved his hand under her top and inched closer to one firm breast.

"Don't!" Skyler cried, trying to pull her arms free, but only helping him in achieving his goal.

"Why?" he asked, as his hand drew closer to her breast, and he touched the underside with his fingertips. "You're so perfect for me."

Adrian let go of her wrists, removed his hand from under her top, flipped her on her stomach, and pulled the tie of her robe off. He used gentle force as he fought to hold her down while he worked on the robe next, jerking it from her body.

"You rotten bag of shit!" Skyler screamed, kicking her legs up as much as she could. "No good sleazebag! Get your goddamn hands off me before I shove your balls down your throat." She managed to turn herself over to her back and slap him a few times before he was able to pin her wrists down. "You suck!"

Adrian laughed. "Is that so?" He fought to get her back to her stomach in order to tie her wrists together.

"What are you doing?" Skyler cried, her fear evident when she kicked her legs. "Adrian! Damn it, stop!"

"Nope, not this time." Adrian pulled her up to the headboard and secured her wrists to it.

"You dirty motherfucker!" she cried, trying to kick at him but hitting nothing.

When Adrian was sure she was not going anywhere, he sat back on his knees to gawk at her. He let his eyes roam over her body and took in the sight before he slowly pushed her top up over her breasts for his first real look. "So perfect," he whispered, running his knuckles over her standing nipples. "You don't know how special you are to me, Skyler." He let his knuckles run down her breasts to her stomach and over her panties. "But you're going to know real soon."

Chapter Three

Skyler wasn't sure what she should do. No one had ever touched her so intimately, let alone tied her to a bed to do it, and the last person she didn't want doing it was Adrian. She was still mortified over her admission that she had wanted to be that girl in the woods with him, not her friend. It was bad enough that his presence in the house caused her to have to fight her feelings for him, but for her to allow her anger to get the best of her and to have let those words slip out was the worst thing that could have ever happened. Now look where she was.

Letting anger get the best of her again had led to her being tied to a bed, with the one man who had all the power in the world to break her heart again hovering over her. She watched his hands trail over her body. It was impossible to suppress the moans or the tremors that quickly came. Finally, Adrian was touching her, and she should be enjoying it. Instead, she was fighting to the end. When Adrian reached her legs, Skyler did everything she could to move away from his touch, including kicking at him, but she had no luck getting away. Adrian was going to touch her no matter what she tried to do.

Adrian leaned over, and she thought he was going to kiss her tummy, but he didn't, he just rubbed his face across it. Skyler couldn't stop the sound of her deep rasping breath, nor could she stop her pussy from becoming wet. His touch felt so good that all of her nerves were alive and screaming for more.

"Do you know how bad I want you right this very second?" he asked her, his voice rough while he rubbed his cheek over her belly. "How easily I could drive you crazy with need?" He kissed her belly, licking right up to her breasts. "How much pleasure I can give you?"

Fearful of how she would sound when she spoke, Skyler didn't answer him. She held her breath and waited to see what he would do next. She was torn. A part of her wanted him to go on, to take the choice from her hands, and the other half wanted him to stop before he finished breaking what was left of her heart. When she peered down at him, Adrian looked up at her and darted his tongue out to lick her nipple just before he sucked it into his mouth. That did it.

"Let me go," Skyler rasped. "Please, Adrian."

Adrian let the nipple he was sucking on pop out of his mouth. "Not yet." He licked the underside of the other breast, as his free hand moved down her body to play with the waistline of her panties.

"This is not fair," Skyler panted.

"But this is the only way I'm going to get to touch you right now." His hand slipped inside the back of her panties, touching her and parting the globes of her ass to tease her before moving slowly to the front to cup her pussy.

"Adrian..." Her voice was barely a whisper.

Adrian pulled on her hair just enough to force her head toward him. He kissed her hard, pushing his tongue past her teeth for a deep kiss. While he explored her mouth, he pushed one finger deep inside her pussy. Skyler arched against him when he moved his finger to match the mating of his tongue. She whimpered into his mouth as he bumped her clit with his thumb, giving her an extra pleasurable sensation that she had never experienced before. When another finger joined the first, he broke the kiss, but their lips still touched.

"Do you know how much I want to be there, where my hand is right this minute?" Adrian asked. The raw emotion in his words was unmistakable. "To feel your heat, your tightness wrapped around me, taking me deep inside of your body and making us one."

Skyler closed her eyes as her hips started to move on their own. The pleasure he gave her, and the climbing need, had her mind turning into putty. Deep down, Skyler had known that if she held out and pushed Adrian long enough, he was going to push back. She just hadn't thought he was going to strike like he was doing now. Adrian licked her lips before he plunged his tongue in for another deep kiss as his hand worked up speed and his thumb pressed harder on her clit.

"Tonight, Skyler, I have to have something more than a kiss or a touch." Skyler opened her eyes and looked at Adrian. "I can't let you go, not until we come together in some way."

Skyler closed her eyes and shook her head. "No," she said in a rush.

Adrian pulled one finger out of her pussy only to rub it over the ring of her ass, getting it as wet as he could. "Don't deny what's between us, Skyler."

Skyler opened her mouth to cry out when Adrian pushed one finger into her ass, but not one sound left her. The pleasure mixed with the slight burning was enough to have her on the brink of orgasm.

"You're close, Skyler." Adrian's voice held an edge to it that Skyler had only heard once and that was when he was in the woods having sex with her friend. "I can smell your need and feel your body as it gets close."

Skyler had to close her eyes to fight the pleasure. He moved his fingers in her ass and pussy with such skill that Skyler knew if he didn't stop soon, she was going to come.

"You like this?" He licked her ear, which sent chills down her spine. "Oh, Skyler," Adrian purred. "I have so much more to show you, and you're going to love it all." Adrian kissed her one more time, brushing his lips across hers. "I want to be inside of you badly." His voice caressed her as only a lover's could. "Do I get my wish, Skyler? Can I have a taste of heaven?"

"You're out of your mind," she finally said.

He answered her with a smile.

Skyler was having a damned hard time thinking while he moved his fingers in and out of her pussy and ass. It felt so good, his possession of her body, but she couldn't deny that it was also a possession of her heart and soul—something she wasn't ready to give.

Adrian sat back up on his heels, removed his fingers from her, and cupped her breasts before letting them go. Running his hands down her stomach, he took hold of the side of her panties, hooking them under his thumb.

"Adrian." Skyler swallowed the lump that had formed in her throat. She was scared, nervous, and excited all in the same bundle. Never had her body felt as tense and on edge as it was now. "What are you going to do?"

Adrian smiled at her. "I'm going to taste you." His voice was calm, his eyes steady. It was enough to have her shaking with the need to experience all that he promised.

Skyler looked at Adrian, her eyes opened wider than she had thought she could ever manage. "You can't be serious."

"Oh, I am." With a yank, he ripped her panties right off.

Trying to free herself, Skyler gave a tug on her arms. "Let me go!" She started to struggle with everything she had inside her. If Adrian was going to do something to her, she sure as hell wasn't going to experience it tied to the fucking bed. "You can't do this to me tied up."

"First, my feast." Adrian took hold of the inside of her thighs and leaned down to her pussy. "Then, your freedom." He darted his tongue out and took one long lick. "Oh, so good."

She wasn't able to speak when his thumbs parted her pussy lips and his mouth went in for more. Skyler squirmed and groaned softly as he licked at her like a cat did milk.

"Oh God, Adrian." Skyler moaned, closing her eyes. "What are you doing to me?"

"I'm loving you," he told her, his voice deep.

Adrian gave her a deep growl and circled her clit with his tongue. She felt his hand open her up, exposing all her secrets to his view. His lips closed around her clit, and his free hand pushed two fingers deep inside. This pushed Skyler over the edge. She cried out, tried to muffle the sounds, but with Adrian still sucking on her, fucking her with his fingers, it was a damned hard thing to do. Her orgasm slammed over her like tidal waves, crashing into her over and over again.

One orgasm after another he gave her before Skyler begged him to stop. Perspiration covered her forehead and chest, and she couldn't catch her breath. Never had she felt so sensitive between her legs.

Finally, when he stopped licking and sucking on her pussy, Adrian laid his head down on her pelvic bone while his hands went up to release her wrists. His heavy breathing matched hers. He said nothing, only tugged on the bindings until both wrists were free, but he kept half of his body still on top of her.

"Are you going to let me up?" she asked, her voice strained and weak. Skyler heard her voice, but almost didn't recognize it. Within the past few nights, Adrian had done everything he could to prevent her from sleeping, and with the orgasm she had just had, she felt as if she could sleep for a week.

"I need more," Adrian told her, with words so thick he sounded like a stranger.

* * * *

Adrian pushed off her and quickly took hold of her legs, dragging Skyler with him to the edge of the bed. He stood up, flipped her over onto her stomach with her legs hanging off the edge, and pinned her between the bed and his body. Adrian knew deep down that he should wait to do what he was about to do until he gave Skyler a bit more experience, but the animal side in him wasn't going to wait. It had to take something and claim it right now.

"What the hell are you doing?" He could hear her panic, but Adrian ignored it. Using most of his body weight to hold her down, he reached under the bed and dragged out his bag of toys

"I love you, Skyler," Adrian told her softly, rubbing his face on her back as he held her close to him by her hips.

Skyler shook her head. "You don't love me. You only want what you can't have."

Adrian heard the pain in her voice, and it tore at his heart. "If I didn't care, would I have made sure you experienced exquisite pleasure?" He slid one hand from her waist and settled it between her legs. He began to rub against her pussy. "Even though I can feel how bad your body wants to be one with mine." He kissed her shoulder, licking at the light mark he had left when they were in the kitchen. "Don't fight what's between us. Don't fight this."

He pushed two fingers as deep as he could inside her and enjoyed how she arched against him and sucked air into her lungs. "Let me move you," he whispered in her ear as he moved his fingers in and out. "Let us both enjoy each other as it's meant to be."

He kept moving his fingers, and when he thought she was close to going over the edge, Adrian stopped all movements. He waited a few seconds before starting it all over again only to stop again.

"Damn it!" Skyler panted. "Stop."

"Together or not at all," he growled. "For your pleasure, I want something." He licked her ear. "And I can do this all night long if I have to. I can keep you on the edge and never let you come."

"Adrian, please." He heard the frustration in her plea.

"Give me this, Skyler." Adrian couldn't keep the pleading out of his voice. "Please, just this."

She hung her head and nodded slightly, and Adrian took it as the yes he wanted. He brought out the baby oil and poured a large amount onto his hand and rubbed it along his cock, preparing before he pushed two fingers as far as they would go into her ass. Skyler cried out, and her back arched, but that didn't stop Adrian from lubricating her as much as he could.

"Adrian!" Skyler panted when he bumped the head of his cock against the small ring of her ass. "It's not going to work."

He didn't answer her. He only spread the globes of her ass to watch as he claimed one part of her body for himself. Adrian pushed as gently as he could, but with enough force to make the ring give in to him. Skyler cried and Adrian blocked it all, focusing all of his attention on the task at hand.

"Relax, relax, oh fuck relax," Adrian moaned. The intense pleasure of her ever-so-tight ass gripping his cock was almost painful. "Motherfucker, you are tight."

"I can't, I can't, I can't," Skyler begged, which sounded more like a pant to him. She was gripping the covers of the bed so tightly that her knuckles turned white, and she pushed back slightly against him. "It's too much."

With one quick thrust, he buried his cock into her ass, and almost lost it all. Close to his own orgasm, Adrian knew this would be a quick ride.

"Get ready for the ride, sweetness," he purred in her ear. "I'm going to rock your world."

Her answer was a moan and to clamp down on him.

Adrian held onto her hips and pulled his cock out slowly. He pushed back in just as slowly, biting his lips and whimpering slightly at the tightness that wrapped around his cock like a fist stroking him to pleasure. Skyler was everything he wanted and more, and this was the first step to his claiming that he was going to take this day.

Claiming Skyler

In and out, he slid his cock, bringing not only himself but also Skyler one step closer to the pleasure that awaited them. He sensed her ecstasy, could smell it rising with his and hear it with the grunts and moans that came out of her mouth. She didn't have to say anything. Her body was saying it all.

"I'm close, Skyler." Adrian moaned, closing his eyes as he picked up the pace. "So fucking close."

Adrian pushed two fingers into her pussy, fucking her with his left hand to match the rhythm of his cock in her ass. Skyler's moans, pleas, and cries got louder with each thrust, each sweet assault he gave her. With a pinch to her clit, Adrian pushed Skyler into an orgasm that triggered his own mind-blowing release. She screamed, and her body clamped down on him. It was enough for Adrian.

Adrian yelled, his cock erupting hot and heavy inside her and filling Skyler to the point of overflowing. Before the last spurt of his seed, Adrian closed his mouth onto her shoulder and bit down hard. The pain brought on another orgasm for her, which heightened his aftershocks of bliss.

Adrian rested against her back, let go of her shoulder and placed his face against hers. He inhaled the sweet scent of her hair. When he opened his eyes, Adrian grinned and dropped to the side of the bed, taking Skyler with him. Skyler bore his mark, finally. There wasn't anything Dedrick or the rest of the fucking male population could do about it. Adrian bit his lower lip as he slid out of her and rolled onto his back. He couldn't stop the smile that slowly spread over his face and felt no shame at being with her or tricking her into it.

* * * *

"You all right?"

Skyler kept her back to Adrian, even when he asked the question. How could she tell him that she was fine, great even? How could she face him when she also felt so ashamed of herself for letting him do what he had just done to her?

She closed her eyes, willing her feelings away and silently cursing the tears. She wasn't hurt. Her body felt alive and relaxed. It was her heart that felt ready to burst and spill all of her secrets to him. As much as she knew she should back off and try to let her wounds heal, she couldn't. Skyler couldn't give him what he wanted. She couldn't accept his claim when he had been with her friend all those months ago.

"Skyler?" His warm hand touched her shoulder and rolled her onto her back.

Skyler pushed her shame aside and slapped him across the face. "Damn you!" she cried, slapping him again before he could get his arms completely around her, stopping her from fighting. Skyler struggled harder and finally got off the bed with the sheet.

"I'm sorry." Adrian sighed, sitting up in the bed.

Backing away, she wrapped the sheet around her body. "Don't. We both know that you're not." She watched him rub his face with his right hand.

"What do you want me to say?"

"I don't want you to say anything!" she cried. "I want you to go back to being my brother's best friend, the guy who wanted nothing more from me than a sisterly friendship. I want *this* to go away." She motioned with her hand around the room.

"It doesn't work that way." Adrian murmured. "We both know that."

"This isn't the old way, Adrian." Skyler took a deep breath and a couple more steps back. "You don't get to come into the home, stake your claim, and we all go live happily ever after."

He cocked his head to one side and frowned. "No, but by rights, in our laws, I can take you from your home if I want. I'm not trying to invoke the old ways here, Skyler. If I did, you would have been under me the first night I was here, or we would be long gone. I'm not the prick you're trying to make me out to be!"

"I don't have to make you out to be anything." She swallowed hard, and she stopped holding back the pain she felt. Skyler did nothing to stop the tears from falling and lowered her voice. "You're doing that all by yourself."

"I didn't know!" Adrian rolled over to the other side of the bed, grabbed his shorts from the floor, and jerked his legs into them.

"You didn't care," she told him softly.

"I care more than you know." With the bed between them, Adrian turned to her with his hands on his hips. "I felt something that night. I felt this raw need inside me that wouldn't go away. Your friend came along at the same time, and yes, I fucked up, but if I had any idea that you were my mate, I would never have gone out there with her."

"But you did!" she yelled. "You went out there and had sex with her, and right after you were finished, you went to *my* brother and put a claim on *me*! What kind of male does that?" Her shoulders shook with her sob.

"Skyler…"

She put her hand up, stopping him from saying any more. "I can't deal with this. I'm going back to my room to try to get some sleep."

Skyler left the room quickly and ran back to hers, and with each step she took, more tears fell down her face to mix with her pain. As much as she hated to admit it, her heart was already in Adrian's hands. What he did to her tonight should have been embarrassing, but it wasn't. In fact, her body screamed that she go back into his room and finish the claim. The only thing that stopped her was the voice in her head reminding her that she couldn't trust Adrian Laswell.

* * * *

Adrian stood in the kitchen with just a cup of coffee in his hand. In the other room, the buffet table was filled with scrambled eggs, bacon, and toast. After last night, he didn't have much of an appetite. Dedrick was sitting at the dining room table reading the newspaper, and Natasha was there also, eating, but Adrian couldn't seem to bring himself to go in and join them. He kept thinking about what happened the night before and how he had placed his mark on Skyler. Guilt for his actions was something Adrian wasn't used to, and he didn't like the taste it left in his mouth. He heard Natasha then.

"Morning, dear."

Adrian felt himself come alive again when he sensed and caught the scent of Skyler as she walked into the room. He didn't leave the kitchen but stayed, leaning against the counter, listening to mother and daughter.

"Is something wrong?" Natasha asked. Adrian sipped his coffee, making no sound. "You look tired. Were you and Adrian fighting all night? I thought I heard shouting."

"I'm fine, Mother." He heard the weariness in her voice. It was just another thing for him to feel guilty about. "Didn't sleep well last night."

"Ma, I'm going to have to go into the city to get some of the things you want for this party," Dedrick said.

"Good." Natasha smiled. "You can pick Jaclyn up from the airport since Sidney isn't feeling well."

Dedrick groaned. "Come on."

"I would do it, but I have to go deal with the caterers," Natasha replied. "So you can pick her up."

Adrian chose that moment to stroll from the kitchen into the dining room with his coffee in his hand. "I can do it." He shrugged.

"Thank you, Adrian," Natasha said with a smile, "but Dedrick can do it. Besides, I think you should stay close and work things out here."

"There's nothing to work out," Skyler retorted dryly. She lowered her voice so Adrian could barely hear, but he did make out the word prick.

Adrian licked his lips and grinned at her. "Something to say, sweetheart?" He finished the last bit of his coffee and then put the cup down hard on the table.

"I have nothing to say to you," Skyler said, giving him a thin smile.

"Are you sure?" The humor of his question was apparent, and he hoped that Skyler would rise to his dare. He wanted to see if she was going to do the same thing she had last night and open her mouth without thinking. "Because I still have plenty to say to you, but not sure if we should do this in front of your family again." He cocked his head to one side and raised an eyebrow. "Unless you're hoping Dedrick will cut my nuts off or something?"

"Adrian!" Natasha gasped.

"Right now, I would *love* to cut them off," Dedrick growled, his eyes suddenly flashing red.

"Dedrick!" Natasha cried this time, silencing them both. "That's enough."

Both stopped, but Dedrick still had the look in his eyes that told Adrian he wanted to rip out his throat.

"Well, a room full of testosterone is not appealing to me." Skyler pushed away from the table. She smiled at Natasha. "I'm going to take a bath." She glared back at Adrian. "There's an itch to my skin that I need to wash off."

Adrian chuckled. "Oh, baby, that hurts." She glared at him before turning her back on him. "I'll be up later to wash your back for you."

Skyler flipped him off, and he laughed but stopped quickly when Natasha gave him a dirty expression.

"What in the world is going on here?" Natasha asked, her eyes going back and forth between them.

Adrian smiled again. "Ask Dedrick." He stepped away from the table. "I'm just following his orders and staking my claim before Friday."

"Dedrick!" Natasha practically squeaked the name out. "You did what?"

"Excuse me." Adrian gave his best charming smile. "I have to go and finish my claim now." He walked away from the table but stopped at the doorway. "Oh, and by the way, Dedrick, I put my mark on her this morning. So my part is pretty much done. Now you get rid of Thomas."

Adrian could hear Natasha yelling at Dedrick until he was halfway up the stairs. He should have felt pity for him, but he didn't. Dedrick had pushed him into a corner, and it was only fitting that Natasha knew about it.

Adrian was very surprised to find Skyler's bedroom door unlatched, especially after what he had done to her that morning. Initially, she'd been hesitant to venture into the kind of sex he so enjoyed, but she'd relented. She couldn't help herself. He wouldn't allow it, and she'd given in. He frowned as he wondered why she had allowed him to take her as he had. She'd been pissed at him still, there was no doubt, yet she'd relented. Then he smiled. Why would she turn him away when he'd carried her to heaven and back, pulling orgasm after orgasm from her?

As quietly as he could, Adrian slipped into her room and closed the door behind him. In the other room, he could hear music playing softly, but no water, so he suspected that she was soaking in the tub. He grinned at the thought, and knowing how Natasha had designed the house, the tub that Skyler was soaking in was probably large enough to hold five.

Stripping, Adrian tossed his clothes on her vanity chair with a grin, even as his cock sprang back to life. As quietly as he could, Adrian opened the bathroom door and slipped inside. Sure enough, the tub in which Skyler bathed was more the size of a swimming pool than a tub. It also had jets that now ran at full blast.

The tub was on the left and, with her back to the door, she apparently hadn't heard him enter. Perfect. For a few minutes, he just stood there looking down at her while she soaked with her eyes closed. The mark on her shoulder shined in his eyes—she was perfect for him in every way.

"You started without me."

Skyler jumped when he spoke. She covered her chest and quickly turned in the tub, moving away from him. "What...what are you doing in here?" she asked, sounding fragile and shaky.

Adrian smiled and slowly swung his leg over the side of the tub. He enjoyed how her eyes raked over his body several times. On purpose, he stood in the tub, letting her get as much of a full view of his body as she could before he lowered into the hot water.

"I'm going to take a bath with you." He stretched his legs out and rested his arms on the sides. "What's it look like I'm doing? I did promise to wash your back for you."

"Adrian, I want to be alone." She obviously tried to sound stern, but it came off as scared to him.

"I want to be with you," he said, trying to charm her.

Skyler rolled her eyes and blushed. "You already have."

Adrian smiled and licked his lips. "Oh, that was only the icing on my cake. Now, I want the rest."

She squirmed, looked around, and kept her hands covering those luscious mounds that caused his mouth to water for her ripe flesh.

"Adrian, I really think you should leave."

Adrian grinned and slowly moved forward, closer to her. He didn't touch, but he did crowd her slightly. "Why?"

"Look, you've done your damage." She shifted in the water, appearing so uncomfortable that he almost felt sorry for her. "I have your damn mark on my shoulder, so why don't you leave me alone?"

"So you think that because I have put my mark on you that it's over?" He kept his voice even and tried to keep his hands to himself. "Because it's not."

Claiming Skyler

"Isn't that how the game is played?" Her sarcasm was back full force. "You chase, you mark, end of story."

"I'm not playing a game here, Skyler. For your information, you are the only one I've ever marked." She snorted and Adrian moved. He grabbed hold of her legs and pulled her onto his lap. "I'm in this for life, Skyler. I'm never going to let you go, and I am going to try like hell never to hurt you like I did that night." She turned her head away from him, but Adrian forced her to look back. "I'm sorry." His voice dropped in tone and all the humor was lost. Adrian spoke from his heart and he wanted Skyler to see it. "I never meant for you to get hurt by my actions."

"I can't trust you," she finally said.

"I know, but one day you will. I promise you that." He smiled, kissed her lightly on the lips, and brushed some of her hair away from her face. "I'm going to do everything I can to earn your trust."

"Well, sneaking into my room and bath is not the best way to earn anything."

Adrian grinned. "Well, the door was unlocked, so I couldn't very well pass up the invite, now, could I?"

"I didn't leave the door unlocked, and let me go."

"The door was cracked open, so you might have locked it, but you didn't shut it all the way." He gave her a big smile. "I'm never going to let you go. We have something to finish." He shifted her on his hips, making sure his cock rubbed between the slit of her pussy.

"Adrian, I don't want to do this," Skyler said, moving her hands from her breasts to his shoulders in an attempt to push him away.

"We won't do any more today." He sighed, holding her tighter and closer. "I just want to hold you. Have you in my arms."

"But, I...um..." She blushed, lowering her eyes.

Adrian chuckled. "Oh, you thought I came into your bath to have sex, huh?" He smiled. Adrian couldn't help it. Her uncertainty and bashfulness made him proud. It was good to know that Skyler didn't mess around with just anyone. "Well, I won't lie to you. I do want to have sex with you, but I can wait if you let me hold you and touch you."

"But, you're going to...um...you're going to want to finish this right?" She blushed again.

"We *are* going to finish this." He rubbed one hand up and down her back. "You have my mark now, so that will be sufficient for everyone. As far as the rest of the world is concerned, you're my mate. They don't need to know about the rest."

"Will you do something for me?" Skyler asked, giving him a sweet smile.

"Depends."

"Can you at least let me take a bath alone?"

Adrian laughed. "Well since you asked me so nicely, I will, under one small condition." He kissed at the mark again, enjoying how she shivered in his arms.

"That would be what?"

"You sleep in the same bed as me," he purred in her ear.

"God, it had to be that." Skyler groaned. "Adrian I don't think..." She trailed off with his movements.

Adrian kissed her on the cheek quickly before getting out of the tub and wrapping a towel around his waist. He wasn't going to point it out, but what had just happened was a major step. For Skyler to not give an unequivocal 'no' to sleeping in the same bed with him was huge, and he planned on doing everything he could to keep going forward and not take any steps back.

"I promise to be a gentleman," he told her as he knelt on the side of the tub and rested his chin on his arms.

Skyler snorted. "Like that will ever happen."

"Okay, I promise for a few days then."

Turning in the tub, Skyler faced him. "This doesn't mean you're out of hot water. I'm still pissed at you."

He leaned over and kissed her on the nose. "That's why I love you. You make a guy work for it."

"You don't love me, Adrian," she said, giving him a grin that was anything but sweet. "You only love the idea of having a good girl as a mate."

Adrian chuckled. "Well, *mate*, you are anything but a good girl. Remember, I grew up with you." He kissed her quickly on the mouth. "Now I'm going to leave before I take back my word and join you again in that bath."

Claiming Skyler

He kissed her once more, lingering softly on her lips. "I promise to make this right between us," he whispered. "On my life, I vow it."

"Don't make promises you can't keep." Her eyes captured his, and Adrian saw the doubt and lingering pain.

"It's a promise I intend to keep." He brushed her face and touched her wet hair. "Until my last breath."

Chapter Four

Adrian sat at the dining room table laughing with Stefan and Sidney. Natasha was in the kitchen with Skyler, and Dedrick was due back any time with Jaclyn. Stefan was telling stories to Sidney about the things Adrian and he had done as children, one being the baseball game in Natasha's sitting room.

"Adrian here was up to bat," Stefan said, his smile bright. "He hit the ball, and it smashed into my mother's favorite vase."

"And Dedrick called it an out," Adrian put in with his own grin.

"Oh, it was an out all right." Stefan laughed. "Once Dedrick saw which vase got broken, he went after Adrian. Chased him all over the house and almost caught him when mom came walking in the front door with Skyler. We hadn't expected her because she had taken Skyler shopping for school clothes that day, and we thought it was going to be an all afternoon thing."

"Stefan blackmailed me into taking the blame. He ended up getting my best baseball card," Adrian said. "What he doesn't know is that Dedrick still kicked my ass for it, so I didn't get off scot-free."

"If he hadn't kept it a secret, you wouldn't have lost your card," Natasha said.

She glided into the dining room with a large plate of pork chops and another plate of baked potatoes. Skyler was right behind her with bowls of salad and mixed vegetables.

Adrian saw the surprised looked on Natasha's face when Skyler sat down next to him. "Well, I didn't want you mad at me," he told Natasha.

"Yet, you took on Dedrick." Natasha shook her head, but smiled at him. "Brave boy."

"God, what is taking him so long?" Sidney sighed, squirming in her chair."

"Well, from what I've seen of your friend," Adrian grinned. "I'm sure she's driving him nuts, and it serves him right."

"Jacy isn't that bad," Sidney said. "She's just outspoken."

"I'll say." Dedrick stormed into the dining room acting like a man who had been through a battle and lost. "That woman can drive the craziest man sane." Giving them all a dirty look, he sat down hard in his chair.

"And you're fucking Prince Charming," Jaclyn snapped back as she sauntered into the dining room.

"Jacy!" Sidney cried with a smile. She jumped from her seat, rushed to the other woman, and hugged her tightly.

Jaclyn Davis was a five-foot-three spitfire with long, sin-black hair that reached her waistline, sparkling blue eyes, and sensual lips. She was a firecracker in Adrian's eyes, one who he enjoyed watching as she kept everyone around her on their toes.

If she had been born a shifter female, she would have been pursued until she dropped. With her narrow hips that rounded out to her legs, and breasts that always seemed to overflow her shirts, she was the kind of woman considered of great worth, strong and proud. Sort of like Skyler, in his opinion.

"Oh, I've missed you," Sidney said, standing back but not letting Jaclyn go.

"Look at you!" Jaclyn said, smiling brightly. "I must say that married life is agreeing with you." She peeked over Sidney's shoulder at Stefan. "You treating her right?"

"Like a goddess," Stefan answered.

"You better." Jaclyn hugged Sidney one more time before taking a seat.

"So, Dedrick's giving you hell, huh?" Adrian asked, leaning back in his chair and draping his arm over the back of Skyler's.

"Him?" Jaclyn pointed her thumb in Dedrick's direction. "Please." She rolled her eyes. "He's a kitten trapped in a bear's body."

Dedrick growled low, and Natasha chuckled. "I don't think I've heard him called that before," she said.

Jaclyn turned to Dedrick. "What the hell is up with all that growling shit?"

Dedrick looked up and frowned. In all the years Adrian had spent in the Draeger home, he couldn't recall once when someone had talked to Dedrick the way Jaclyn did.

"You trying to pull that wolf shit on me, 'cause let me tell you something, I'm not Red Riding Hood, and you're no damn badass."

Adrian spit out his drink and smiled at the shock that crossed Dedrick's face or rather the tick that started in his cheek. There weren't too many who had the balls to speak to Dedrick in anything but fear or respect, so for Jaclyn to say what was on her mind in front of everyone took a lot of courage.

"Do you know he wouldn't stop growling the whole trip here?" Jaclyn went on, grinning at Sidney. "I swear, if I didn't know better, I would think he needed to get laid or something."

That was it. Adrian started to choke on his drink, and Stefan and Skyler busted out laughing. Natasha just sat there looking lost for words.

"Oh, this is going to be good," Stefan mumbled to Adrian.

"Priceless." Adrian chuckled.

Natasha cleared her throat. It was obvious she had a hard time not cracking a smile. "So, how long do we have you, dear?"

"Oh, just for a few days," Jaclyn answered. She cast Dedrick another glance, meeting his glare head on. "Don't want to ruffle someone's feathers too much now."

"Excuse me, Mother." Dedrick pushed away from the table with a frown. "I have some work to do."

Adrian burst out laughing as soon as Dedrick was out of the room. "Oh, man." Tears started to come to his eyes as he laughed. "You have *got* to stay longer."

"Just a few days," Jaclyn reiterated. "I promised my mother I would stop by and see her before too long. She said she has something important to tell me, and knowing her, it would be that she needs to borrow money again, or maybe she's marrying that bum she's been dating."

"I thought you were going to stop giving her money?" Sidney said.

"I am." Jaclyn smiled. "I plan on reminding her of that when I get there, but she also said that there is something I need to know, so I might as well get it over with. Give her a few bucks and she goes away as always." She turned to Adrian, and he felt like he was in for it. Jaclyn might be a small woman, but she packed one hell of a punch. "Skyler tells me that you two have mated or whatever you guys call it."

The change of topic was apparent, and Adrian smiled and nodded. "Yes, we did."

"Huh." Jaclyn cocked her head to one side, piercing Adrian with her blue eyes. "Congratulations then."

It's obvious, Adrian thought, casting a glance at Skyler who seemed a little uncomfortable. "It's a little complicated," he added.

"Not judging." Jaclyn smiled. "I know I'm the outsider here but hey!" She hugged Sidney again. "As long as Sidney is happy, I'm happy, and what all is your business is not mine. So don't worry about me spilling the beans. I take secrets to the grave."

"Now, Jaclyn," Natasha handed the plate of pork chops over, "will you be back for the party?" she asked, effectively changing the subject with a smile.

"Oh, I don't know." Jaclyn smiled back. "I don't do well at big fancy parties." She took the food handed to her and passed it along. "All the dress up and stuff."

"I'm sure you'll be lovely," Natasha told her. "I'm not going to take no for an answer." She took hold of Jaclyn's hand. "You are special to Sidney, and therefore important to us. It's important that we all work to be comfortable with each other."

"Skyler can take us shopping." Sidney smiled. "She's great with picking out clothes."

"Only great when I'm spending other people's money," Skyler said.

"Boy, don't I know it," Stefan said under his breath, which got him an elbow in the gut.

"Give her a break," Sidney chastised him. "It was Skyler who picked that red outfit you love so much."

Stefan groaned and covered his face with his hands. "I did not need to know that!"

Jaclyn laughed, turning to Sidney. "So, what's so important that you wanted me to rush into town?"

"Well." Sidney glanced around the room at everyone. From the way she squirmed in the chair, Adrian figured it was something pretty important.

"Should I get Dedrick?" Adrian asked.

"I'm here," he said, sounding as if he'd rather be anywhere but there. "Skyler, you have a call."

Adrian's gut twisted at the way Dedrick looked at her. His expression was hard and disapproving, the kind a father would wear, if his daughter was seeing a boy he didn't like, and the boy came sniffing around. Adrian's instincts were always right when it came to telling him that something was off. The hardness in Dedrick was clearly saying something was up, and he wasn't going to like that something one bit.

"Can you ask whoever it is to call back?" Skyler glanced from Dedrick back to Sidney. "I don't want to miss anything."

"Okay." Dedrick turned back around, left, and came back a few minutes later.

Sidney took a deep breath and smiled at Stefan before looking around the room once more. "Okay, first off, I want to say thanks to you all for making me feel like I'm a part of this family. Even though I have a father, he hasn't been much of anything most of my life, and I'm sorry for everything that he has done and is trying to do to you all. I know that it's been very hard at times for you to accept Jacy, so thanks for doing that as well. I know that what you all are is a major secret, and I trust her to keep it. She has always been a sister to me and, at times, one I wanted to strangle."

Jaclyn grinned and rolled her eyes. Adrian slipped his hand under the table, took hold of Skyler's, and was happy when she didn't pull away from him for a few seconds.

"So, anyway," Sidney went on. "I wanted to have my whole family around for this." She took another deep breath, and Adrian saw her hands shaking on the table. Apparently, she was nervous about something. "I'm pregnant!"

The room went still. Stefan looked like he was about to fall out of his chair. Clearly, Adrian thought, Stefan hadn't known about this.

"Holy shit!" Jaclyn gasped. "You're sure?"

Sidney smiled. "Oh, I'm sure."

"I...I..." Stefan didn't get another word out. He slipped from the chair onto the floor, passed out.

"Stefan!" Sidney and Natasha cried at the same time.

Jaclyn grinned at Adrian, who stood up. "I thought you guys were stronger than this?"

"So did I," Adrian said before he grinned.

Again, dinner had turned out to be a drama scene similar to one you would watch in a soap opera. Dedrick helped Stefan up to his room with Sidney following. Skyler had a call again but wouldn't tell Adrian who it was or what it was about. He kind of guessed that it was Thomas.

Adrian sort of wondered if Dedrick hadn't bothered to call him, or maybe he didn't have the time with all the other stuff going on in the house. Hell, as many summers and weekends as he spent here, he couldn't recall one this crazy, but Adrian still felt that when Dedrick was on the phone with the guy, he should have told him Skyler was no longer available.

Waiting for Skyler, Adrian thought about the past few hours. He had a small truce with her, one that was very rocky. He wasn't stupid. He knew Thomas was after her and wasn't going to let this claim go easy, if that's what one wanted to call it. Adrian's gut was telling him that Thomas was up to no good and not knowing what was going to happen was killing him.

While he waited, Adrian found Dedrick in the kitchen drinking a beer. "Hey, can I talk to you for a few."

Dedrick took a drink and placed his bottle down before glancing at Adrian. "Why not? It's already been one hell of a night."

Adrian didn't bother going over to sit down, but crossed his arms over his chest and thought how he was going say what was on his mind. Deciding it was just better to come out with it, he said, "I don't want Skyler going to the safe house."

Dedrick stopped with the bottle inches from his mouth. "What?"

"I don't want Skyler going to the safe house with your mother," Adrian said again, waiting for Dedrick's anger to boil over like it seemed to do lately.

Dedrick took his drink and nodded. "Your call, but I hope to hell you know what you're doing."

"You and me both." Adrian left the kitchen to go back out and wait for Skyler.

When Skyler came out of the office, Adrian tensed slightly. He watched how her shoulders were slumped, and in a way, she looked defeated.

"Bad phone call?" he asked from his seat on the stairs.

Skyler jumped. "How long have you been sitting there?"

"Long enough," he told her. Adrian braced himself for the fight he knew was about to come. "It was Thomas, wasn't it?"

Skyler squared her shoulders, and the old fire once again lit her eyes. "That's none of your damn business," she snapped. She walked to the stairs, apparently intending to go past him, but Adrian was quicker. He stood and grabbed her arm, stopping her.

"It is my business," he hissed, with his jealousy again rearing its ugly head. "You're my mate."

"I'm very well aware of that," she replied through gritted teeth, trying to yank her arm free. "You made sure you put your damn mark on me."

"Do I need to do it again?" Adrian yanked her closer. "Do you need a reminder, Skyler?"

He knew he sounded almost threatening, but his jealousy wouldn't be subdued. It was the animal part of him. Any threat from another male sniffing around what he considered his could become dangerous. Adrian took a deep breath, letting it out slowly. He reminded himself to go slow, and try to be nice, instead of the bastard he knew he had been, but the thought of Thomas pissed him off.

"What you need to do is let me go and cool off." She managed to get her arm free and put some space between them. "If we're going to try and find middle ground here, you need to trust me." She took a few steps before his cold words stopped her.

"I talked to Dedrick about the safe house thing while you were in his office." Adrian kept his back to her. "You're not going with your mother this time."

"You can't do that." She glared at him, her hands going to her hips.

Adrian slowly turned and had to look up at her since she had taken a few more steps up the stairs. "We're mated, Skyler. Before your cycle kicks in, I will have you completely, so there's no need for you to go there this time."

Skyler didn't say anything to him, but stomped up the stairs to her room and slammed the door. As much as Adrian hated having to force her to stay during her cycle and experience it with him, he had to do this. The sooner she got into the routine of each month by his side the better.

It hurt him deeply that despite the steps he had taken to get closer to her, he had only ended up pushing her away. He slept alone that night, or at least he tried to sleep. Adrian felt like his body was on fire. After having a taste of the passion that was Skyler, Adrian felt like he couldn't breathe unless she was near him, but with her being so pissed off again, there was no chance in hell she was going to let him sleep in the same bed with her.

Adrian gave up trying to sleep around seven in the morning. He quickly showered and dressed in jeans and sleeveless shirt and sneakers. As much as he wanted to, he didn't stop by Skyler's bedroom to check on her. He simply walked past her door and down the stairs.

He was surprised to find that everyone was already up, and Natasha preparing to take Sidney to see a shifter doctor. Stefan and Jaclyn were going to tag along, and they were all gathered in the kitchen when Adrian strolled in.

"Why did you have to make the appointment so damn early, Mom?" Stefan whined, yawning. He nodded when he saw Adrian walk in.

"I didn't," Natasha answered. "I called, and he squeezed us in."

"At eight in the morning?" Stefan yawned again.

"Oh, suck it up," Adrian said, walking over to the coffee pot to pour himself a cup. "You know how rare it is for humans to get pregnant by us."

"Why is it so rare?" Jaclyn asked.

"Something about your DNA," Adrian answered before taking a sip. "To be blunt, shifter sperm doesn't hold much human DNA, so the chance for a human to conceive is very low, whereas a full-blooded female shifter going through her cycle each month is higher. They are fertile and stay that way until after a male goes through his heat, giving a very high chance to conceive."

Jaclyn shook her head and crossed one leg over the other. "You guys are so strange."

Dedrick walked in making a *humph* sound. "Pot calling the kettle black again?"

"Oh, look everyone." Jaclyn's voice was as sweet as the fake smile on her lips. "The big bad wolf has graced us with his presence."

"Keep it up, Jaclyn," Dedrick barked back, "and I'll show you just how bad this wolf can get."

Adrian watched as she licked her lips and let her gaze roam over his frame. Adrian thought that someone needed to tell Jaclyn just how bad Dedrick could be if pushed too far and to back off before it was too late.

"Such promises." She smiled and turned back in her chair to face Natasha. "We had better go if you want to make it on time."

"You're right." Natasha quickly rushed from the room, but stopped at the doorway to look hard at Dedrick and Adrian. "Will you two promise me not to kill each other while we're gone?

"I'll be good," Adrian said in a syrupy sweet voice.

Dedrick grunted. "Go, Mother, before you're late."

Adrian didn't bother to sit down. From the way Dedrick was pacing the kitchen, he knew that something was on his mind. Adrian hoped it wasn't something that was going to start another fight between them. He had enough on his plate with Skyler bucking him at every turn. As much as he hated it, he did need to finish his claim on her before this weekend. It was Thursday now, and the full moon was due Wednesday, which meant Skyler's cycle would start Monday. Not much time for him to fix the problem they had.

"Okay, shoot," Adrian said to Dedrick the moment he heard the door close. "I know there's something on your mind." He placed his cup on the counter and crossed his arms over his chest.

"I called Thomas the other night to tell him what was going on," Dedrick said, sounding strained. Adrian didn't know much about what was going on with the man, but he did know that the coming full moon was starting to take its toll on him.

"And?"

Dedrick took a deep breath. "He wants to fight it. Thinks we have cheated him out of something. He also called Skyler last night to try to talk some sense into her."

"You let her talk to him?" Adrian didn't hide his anger.

"No, I tried to block him," Dedrick growled back. "The fucker called five times—in a row!" He rubbed his face, showing Adrian the lack of and need for sleep. Dedrick was suffering and needed a mate of his own in the worst way.

"Why do I have this feeling that you are about to tell me something I'm not going to like?" Adrian braced himself for the worst and soon discovered he wasn't disappointed.

"Thomas is here." Dedrick sighed. "He came over thirty minutes ago and refused to leave until he spoke to Skyler. They're in the family room, and I think you need to go back there and deal with him."

Adrian took a deep breath, frowning at his new brother-in-law. "You know, Dedrick, I have enough shit going on as it is. Skyler is fighting me on everything I do, including her not going to the safe house, and now you toss this crap at me?" He pushed away from the counter, heading out of the kitchen, but stopped at the doorway to glare at Dedrick. "You were supposed to handle Thomas."

"Adrian, don't act like you're the only one in this house who has problems." The warning was unmistakable. Dedrick followed Adrian out of the kitchen. "I'm trying to protect my family, accept your claim, and deal with my fucking heat!" he snapped. "I tried to handle Thomas, but the handling is going to have to be done by you. You *are* her mate, so fucking deal with it."

"You're all charm, Dedrick," Adrian said over his shoulder.

Adrian walked down the hall to the back family room. He bypassed Natasha's sitting room, went past the stairs, and pushed open the door to the room where he knew Skyler was—with Thomas. He heard the voices before he saw them, but what he heard was enough to get his temper flaring.

"Skyler, please." Thomas Fallen's words could have been heard a mile away. "Come with me. We can dissolve the claim, and you can become my mate instead."

"Thomas, it doesn't work that way, and you know it," Skyler answered. "I'm sorry this has happened, but coming here doesn't change things."

"It can change everything!" Thomas' pitch rose. "We could force your brother to toss Adrian out on his ass where he belongs."

"Kind of hard to do since she has my mark." Adrian strolled into the family room with a grin that he was sure was anything but lighthearted or humorous. When he saw the shocked expression on Thomas's face, Adrian said, "Oh, she didn't tell you, did she?"

"Adrian," Skyler pleaded, looking from him to Thomas.

"I can tell by your face that I'm right." He couldn't stop the smugness. "Want to see it?"

"You're not right for her," Thomas yelled.

If looks could kill, Adrian would have been dead on the spot. It was in that moment that he saw just how much Thomas Fallen hated him. "You're nothing more than a whore in a man's body."

"And you're a girl trapped in a man's body." Adrian laughed.

Thomas lunged at Adrian, but Skyler put herself between them. "Stop! Please!"

"She's taken, Thomas," Adrian said. "So there's no point in you sniffing around any longer."

Skyler turned her head to peek over her shoulder at him. "Will you stop?"

Adrian put one hand on his hip, the other he rubbed around his mouth to his jaw, working at taming his anger. "No, I won't," he snapped back. "This little twig here has been dating you and trying like hell to charm you into his bed when there was a damn claim on you."

"If I would have known that, I wouldn't have dated him," Skyler said through gritted teeth. "I wasn't informed of a claiming until now."

"Once again you show your true colors." Thomas smiled. "Always thinking about yourself first." He crossed his arms over his chest, grinning cruelly. "Does she know about your past? All of it, I mean."

"Does she know about yours?" Adrian took a threatening step.

"My past doesn't involve sleeping with everyone's sister and their friends."

Thomas's face was smug, and that gave Adrian the feeling of nails on a chalkboard. Adrian lunged at him, but Skyler was quick to insert between them again and put her hands on his chest, struggling to hold him back.

"I'm going to rip your fucking throat out!" Adrian yelled, struggling against Skyler to get at Thomas. "You're a goddamn worthless excuse for a shifter male!"

Claiming Skyler

Dedrick rushed into the room. "Thomas, it's time for you to leave," he informed the man.

"I was just leaving." Thomas grinned. He smiled at Skyler, and Adrian wanted to kill the man. "We'll finish this discussion later."

"There isn't anything to be finished, you fuck!" Adrian yelled.

"The claim stands, Thomas," Dedrick said. "I'm not dissolving it. Now please leave."

Thomas glared once more at Adrian. "It's not over with." He turned and walked out of the room with Dedrick following.

Skyler pushed Adrian away from her, turned her back, and walked over to a window, putting as much space between them as she could. "I could have handled that."

Adrian snorted. "Thomas is a damn snake, Skyler. Slippery as they come and scared of his own damn shadow. How in the hell you got involved with him, I'll never know."

"Stay out of it, Adrian!" she snapped. "He doesn't concern you."

"Doesn't concern me?" Adrian frowned. "Have you lost your mind? Everything about you concerns me! You're my damn mate, Skyler."

"How can I forget? You're down my throat all fucking day long!" She covered her eyes with one hand and took several deep breaths. "Adrian, I need time to understand all of this." She looked at him, pleading with her blue eyes. "I need time to understand what's going on here."

"You need time." He bit his lower lip, nodding, feeling the frustration over the whole situation. "We don't have time, Skyler. Don't you understand that?"

"Damn it, listen to yourself!" she cried.

"Oh, I am listening." He spoke through his teeth, feeling his anger rise with each breath. "I heard your *boyfriend*," he let the word slide from his tongue with venom, "has been trying to claim you for months when you were already claimed. I heard you talking to him all soft and sweet, and I wish like hell it was me!"

Breathing hard, he took a step. "Six months I've waited, fighting with myself to stay away and give you time to adjust to this. I've tried to back away when you asked me, slept alone when you should have been by my side, and what do *I* get? I get to find you in here, alone with him!

So please, tell me when the hell I am allowed to be pissed off and hurt here."

"Yes, it's all about Adrian. Again, for your damn information, I didn't know about the fucking claim six months ago!" she shouted back. Adrian winced at her brattiness. "But hey, let's all bow down and give Adrian what the hell he wants and be grateful for it." She rolled her eyes at him. "Grow up, Adrian. This world does not revolve around you."

"Oh, I don't want the world, Skyler." His tone dropped. "I just want you."

She shook her head. "I can't do this, not with you so angry."

"Angry?" Adrian chuckled. "Oh, I'm not angry, maybe a little upset to find Thomas here." He moved both of his hands to his hips, frowning at her. "What I'm tired of is all this bullshit between us."

"Too bad." Her hands went to her waist, and she faced off with him. The defiance she showed became an instant turn on for Adrian. "I'm not one of your bimbos who will crumble at your feet and beg like hell for some attention. I didn't ask for this, Adrian. So, if you want me, like you claim you do, you're going to have to go at my pace. End of story."

Adrian narrowed his eyes. "You know, you're right," he said. "It is the end of the story, right now."

"Adrian, what are you doing?" Skyler took a step back as he came forward.

"I already told you." He grinned. "I'm ending this."

Skyler made a quick turn to run up the stairs, but Adrian was quicker. "Not this time." He grabbed for her waist, but she kept ahead of him. "You're not running from it this time."

"Adrian, please," she cried. "You need to calm down."

"Oh, I'm calm." He stalked toward her, forcing her back into the room again. "For the first time where you're concerned, I'm real fucking calm."

"What the hell is going on now?" Dedrick came rushing into the foyer to glare up at the two of them.

"Dedrick!" Skyler cried. "Help me get this animal off me!"

"Stay the fuck out of it, Dedrick," Adrian snapped. He wound his hands around her waist and plucked her right off her feet.

"Dedrick!" Skyler squealed. "Aren't you going to do something?"

"Not this time," Adrian answered with a growl. "This time, it's between you and me."

* * * *

"Get your fucking hands off me!" Skyler struggled with everything she had to escape his grip on her, to no avail.

Of all the things for Adrian to do, Skyler never thought he would manhandle her again. She tried to hold onto the top banister of the stairs, but Adrian used his strength to pry her fingers away. She tried to kick back at him, but once again, Adrian used that damn strength of his and hauled her over to his left hip like a bag of potatoes.

"Keep it up, Skyler." He grunted when she landed an elbow in his gut. "You're only making this worse for yourself."

"Go to hell!" she screamed.

She fought him with more force when he reached her bedroom door. Skyler did everything she could to stop him from opening it and even almost managed to get out of his hold, but it seemed that luck was on Adrian's side and not hers. He forced Skyler into her room, kicked the door closed, and pinning her against it face-first while he locked it. Roughly, he turned her around, and Skyler saw an Adrian she didn't know.

"I never thought you would put me in a position like this." Adrian growled and slammed his hands on the door, causing her to jump.

"I haven't done anything to you," she yelled back, suddenly feeling caged. "You're the one that has come into my life and turned it upside down."

"Is that so?"

Skyler could see the tick in his cheek, but instead of keeping her mouth shut as she should have, she went on. There was no way in hell she was going to let him bully her.

"Yes, that's so." She pushed at his chest, but Adrian didn't move. "Everything was just fine until you showed up with your damn claim. Did you even think about how I felt about that? Do you even give a fuck?" she yelled in his face. "I don't want this, Adrian. I don't want some guy who thinks he's a fucking Don Juan stud as my mate, so that means I don't want you!"

"Well too damn bad," he answered her all too calmly. "I made my claim, Skyler, and I'm not going away. You can rant, be pissed, and throw all the tantrums you want, but I'm not leaving."

Skyler screamed and did the one thing she knew would come back and bite her in the ass later. She pushed her knee as hard as she could into his nuts. "You fucking bastard!"

Skyler pushed him away, unlocked the door, and ran out. Down the stairs she went until she ran into Dedrick, who was coming out of his office reading some papers.

"Jesus, Skyler." Dedrick groaned and his papers fell to the ground. "What the hell is going on now?" They both looked up at Adrian who was slowly walking down the stairs holding his groin. "Son of a bitch!" Dedrick whispered to Skyler, who was trying to put himself between the two. "What did you do now?"

"No one owns me or controls me, Adrian," Skyler said from behind Dedrick. "You need to get used to that right now!"

"Adrian?" Dedrick asked with caution. "What's going on?"

"I…am…going to kill her," he groaned, looking like he was in major pain. "That's what's going on."

"Adrian, you need to calm down," Dedrick said, trying to shield Skyler as best as he could.

Skyler watched Adrian. Sure enough, he had murder in his red eyes. She knew she should have thought about what she was going to do before she did it, but being manhandled didn't fly with her. Skyler had never been treated like that, even when her brothers and mother were pissed off at her. So seeing how angry Adrian was at that moment, she knew that being alone with him wasn't a good idea.

"When I get my hands on her," Adrian growled, flashing a cold, red stare, "I am going to beat her until she admits that she's mine!" He huffed his words out. "And then before this night is out, I'm going to finish my claim."

"Letting your temper overrule here won't help things," Dedrick told him.

"No, letting her continue to act like she can control this isn't helping," Adrian snapped. He tried to lunge at her, but Skyler was faster.

"Oh, what's wrong, Adrian?" *Shut up, Skyler*, she said in her head.

Just shut the fuck up and walk away. "This little girl getting the upper hand? Is that the only way you can feel important or like a man? Does it take having some girl on her knees before you?" *Now you've done it.*

The red in his eyes brightened. The tick in his cheek worked faster, and he began to huff and puff.

"Now leave me the hell alone, or I'm going to kick your nuts all the way up to your goddamn throat!"

Adrian made another lunge, but again, Skyler was quicker. She moved around Dedrick but also backed away.

"I have a better idea," Adrian growled. "Why don't I put my—"

"That's enough!" Dedrick bellowed.

"You're right." Adrian panted. "It is enough. You want your space? Fine, you've got it." Seconds seemed to tick by with the two of them glaring at each other, Dedrick standing between them. "You've got your time."

"Just like that?" Skyler was breathing hard from the fight, but she didn't trust him, not as far as she could throw him.

Adrian sniffed, wiped his face and nose, and Skyler could have sworn that she saw tears in his eyes. He nodded. "Just like that."

Skyler watched Adrian walk away from her, his strong shoulders slumped, looking like a man who'd just been beaten down. Watching him leave, guilt hit her in the gut. Instead of being happy that she had gotten what she wanted, she felt bad. She kept her eyes on him as he headed into the kitchen and then jumped when she heard the slamming of the back door. Skyler watched from the back door as he headed to the woods and not the pool house like she thought he would.

"I thought I heard a door slam." Stefan walked into the kitchen a frown on his face. Skyler frowned when she saw Stefan, and he held up his hand. "Mom forgot her purse on the counter so I came back for it," he said as if to answer her question. "Is everything okay?"

Skyler turned and frowned. Adrian was gone from her view, lost in the sunlight and into the woods. "I don't know," she whispered. "I think I've hurt him pretty bad this time."

Stefan moved to stand behind Skyler and placed his hands on her shoulders. "Oh, come on, nothing's as bad as what you might think."

"It was that bad," Dedrick said.

"I think I've pushed him away for good." Skyler sighed. "I didn't think he would give up so suddenly."

"Come on, Skyler," Stefan said. "Adrian's tough. I'm sure you didn't push him away."

"He walked away, didn't he?" Skyler answered in a mumble. "He walked away."

Chapter Five

Skyler walked down the stairs the next morning feeling like something wasn't right but unable to put her finger on it. The whole house seemed extra quiet and full of tension. As she headed for the dining room, she thought about the fight she had with Adrian. Something about it wasn't sitting well with her. He'd given up too easily, way too easily. For a guy who was bent on claiming her in every way possible, to stop and walk away, giving her the space she thought she needed was a turnaround that just didn't feel right.

Breakfast wasn't laid out on the buffet, and Dedrick wasn't in his usual place at the head of the table reading his paper. That alone had the hairs on the back of her neck standing at full attention. She heard her brothers in the kitchen talking and braced herself to face them and Adrian. What a shock! Adrian wasn't in the kitchen with them.

Natasha sat at the kitchen table. Dedrick leaned against one counter and Stefan leaned against one on the other side of the kitchen. The three of them stopped talking when she walked in. She knew right away that they had been discussing her.

"What's going on?" she asked, crossing her arms over her chest.

Natasha looked at Dedrick, and he shrugged at her. "Sit down."

She turned to Dedrick. "What's going on?" she repeated.

"Adrian has requested that you be taken to the safe house until after the full moon," Dedrick answered, his own arms coming up to cross over his chest.

"What?" Skyler couldn't believe her ears. First, he wanted her to stay; now he was making her leave. "Why? I…I don't understand. He told me that I was to stay here this time."

"He's changed his mind."

Skyler didn't like the coldness in her brother's voice or the way he looked at her with disapproval. "He can't do that!"

"He can," Dedrick stated. "And I'm allowing it."

Skyler gawked at her brother. It was like seeing a man she didn't know. When had Dedrick become so hard? She didn't know. "So this is my punishment for not opening my arms to him." She glared at Dedrick. "He tosses me away, and you let him."

"He can't toss you away," Natasha said. "You have his mark, but he does have the right by our law to send you away."

"You all let him!" Skyler yelled.

"He's doing this so that neither one of you will be tempted to seek the other out," Stefan finally said. His hands were stuffed in his pockets, and he had guilt written all over his face. "Adrian is only giving you what you asked for—space."

"By getting that, *he* gets to send me away?" Skyler was pissed off at being sent away from her home, and she was pissed off that Adrian would do this behind her back. Why didn't he come to her and let her know what he was planning? Was this his great plan for giving her the space she asked for? Skyler found that she was taken aback by it all. Hurt, anger, confusion, it all hit her at once. *But this is what you wanted!* A voice in her head screamed. Not like this, she answered. *Adrian isn't giving me space. He's pushing me away.*

"Where is he?" she asked, looking around the room at them all.

"He left," Natasha answered. "Late last night."

Skyler turned and ran from the room, back to the stairs where she took them two at a time. She headed to his room, barging in, not believing that he would leave without saying a word to her. Sure enough, Adrian wasn't in his room, and the bed didn't seem like it had been slept in.

"You wanted this." Dedrick stood behind her. Skyler looked around for something that might tell her where he went. "You asked for space, and he has given it to you."

"Did he move out?" She couldn't turn to her brother, was afraid of what her eyes might tell him.

"No." Dedrick sighed from behind her. "He's going to be gone for the whole day as you pack what you need. Mom wants him to keep staying here since you do have his mark."

Skyler nodded, still keeping her back to him, a tear slipping free.

Space she did want, abandonment she didn't.

"He told me that he would stay, but that you shouldn't worry about him being in your face. He's going to make sure that you don't run into him that much."

More tears fell, which angered her more. "I guess...um...guess I should go pack then."

* * * *

Adrian leaned against his truck, arms crossed over his chest, one ankle over the other watching the house, seeing Stefan and Dedrick carrying bags to the car that waited out front. Natasha and Skyler were heading for the safe house, and it tore his heart apart.

Normally not the kind of male to cry, Adrian did this time while he watched Skyler climb into the car and take off. More tears fell from his eyes than he could count. His beast screamed for him to run and take her, but he just couldn't bring himself to move. He'd lost her. There was no other way he could look at it, except that his mate was lost to him forever. He watched the car until he couldn't see it any longer. Then Adrian slumped to the ground. The pain in his chest was too much to bear. He hugged himself and yelled, letting out all his pain and frustration.

Adrian didn't go back to the house until one in the morning. Staggering in the front door, he felt more out of place inside than he had the first time Stefan brought him over to meet his mother. For the rest of the night, he drank and drank hard, hoping like hell that the booze would help dull the pain in his chest. Instead, what ended up happening was that his head started pounding with the grandfather of all headaches. It matched the horrible ache of his heart.

Somehow, he made it up the stairs without falling, and kept hold of his half-empty bottle of scotch. Adrian closed his eyes as he passed Skyler's bedroom. He tried not to think about her being gone, just like he was trying not to think about all the things he had done wrong. He should never have placed a claim on her. She was too damn good for him. He took a drink from the bottle and opened his bedroom door.

Dedrick was sitting in the corner chair, waiting for him to come back. "Dedrick." Adrian sighed when he glanced up. "Now's not the best time."

"So is this how you're going to handle things?" Dedrick asked, uncrossing his legs and standing up.

"I'm handling things just fine," Adrian told him, surprised that he didn't slur the words.

"Yeah, you're handling this just fine," Dedrick said dryly.

Adrian staggered over to the nightstand, placed the bottle down, and fell onto the bed, face first. "Go away," he mumbled with his face in the covers.

Dedrick grabbed hold of his arms and forced him to roll over. "Getting drunk isn't going to fix this, Adrian."

"It's fixed!" Adrian screamed back. Coming to his feet, he pushed Dedrick away. Quickly, he sobered and glared at the man. "She wanted time. Over and over again that was all she wanted, and that's what I gave her! She got her space, and if it wasn't out of respect for your mother, I would leave and never come back." He charged at Dedrick, grabbed the man by his shirt. "So why don't you leave me the fuck alone." He pushed Dedrick away from him with a snarl. He turned his back on Dedrick, pacing the room, feeling edgy. "I shouldn't have come back here." He stopped his pacing and glared at Dedrick. "I should have kicked your ass for not telling her and left!"

"Are you finished?" Dedrick bellowed back.

"Yeah," Adrian growled. "I'm finished."

"Good. Now sit down and shut the fuck up," Dedrick growled, pointing at the bed.

Adrian gave him another glare before going to the bed and sitting down on the edge.

"I'm not going to stand here and stroke that ego of yours by telling you you're a good guy. You've always been like a bitch in heat, always sniffing for the next girl to sleep with. Skyler saw it, and I saw the way she always looked at you. If you hadn't fucked that girl that night, or if Skyler hadn't seen it, this shit wouldn't be happening now. But it is!"

Adrian opened his mouth to speak, but Dedrick cut him off.

"Let me finish. Giving Skyler this time, I think it's going to be good for both of you. You need to cool off, and she needs the time to think. What I don't think is going to help is you drinking." Dedrick snatched the bottle from the table before Adrian could grab it. "So you do whatever it is you think you need to do, just keep the booze out of it." Dedrick nodded, turned, and headed for the door.

"What if she never accepts me?" Adrian asked, feeling the weight of the world on his shoulders.

Dedrick stopped with his hand on the knob. He didn't turn around when he spoke. "I don't know, Adrian. This time, I don't have the answers."

Adrian spent the rest of the week locked in his room. He didn't come out for meals, didn't answer when Stefan or Sidney knocked on the door asking how he was doing. All he did was sit in a corner, on the floor of his room, defeated. He felt broken, lost, as if his world was crashing down around him. His heat came like it did every month, and it raged in his system with a new demand that was so painful it blurred his vision. Adrian took it all. He didn't move from his corner, didn't cry out. Feeling as if it was the punishment for all the wrongs he'd done Skyler, he just let the pain hit with his need.

* * * *

The morning, it was over, he crawled from his corner into the bathroom and took a shower. As much as it pained him, he felt as if he needed to get out of the house before Skyler came home. He couldn't face her. He couldn't bear to see his heart look back at him with hate and fear. He knew that what he needed to do was let her go, but with his mark on her shoulder, and him alive, it was going to be impossible for Skyler to get herself another mate. Yet still, he was going to let her go. He would no longer pursue her like he had. It was a hard choice, but one he felt was the best for Skyler, and it tore his heart and soul apart. Dressed in clean clothes, Adrian left his room after many days of locking himself in and rushed to the stairs. He didn't want anyone to see him. He knew that despite his shower, he still looked like shit due to lack of food and sleep. He got as far as the foyer before he was spotted.

"Adrian!" Stefan called from the dining room.

As much as he hated to, Adrian stopped, but he didn't turn to Stefan or say anything.

Stefan came out with his napkin in hand. "Where are you going?

Skyler's going to be home soon, man. Don't you want to talk to her?"

Adrian hung his head down. "I know."

"You know?" Stefan sounded surprised. "If you know, why are you leaving?"

Adrian took a deep breath before turning to look at his best friend. "Because it's what she wants."

"Come on, man." Stefan tried to laugh, but one quick glance from Adrian, and he stopped. "Skyler doesn't want you to go away. She's just having a hard time with all this. She's still pissed off, but she'll come around."

Adrian shook his head. "There are some things people can't forgive, Stefan. Skyler can't forgive me for sleeping with her friend and then coming and making a claim on her. It's time I come to terms with it."

Stefan frowned at him. "What are you saying?"

Adrian took another deep breath and faced the door. He jerked it open. "I'm saying that I'm going to have to let go as much as I can. My mark is on her, so my claim is intact, and I'll stay here to save face, but as far as finishing it...I'm not going to."

"You can't be serious."

Adrian saw the car turn into the long drive, and the pain of his decision hit. "Yeah, I am." He walked out, not giving Stefan time to say another word. As quickly as he could, he rushed to his truck.

On his way down the drive, he passed Natasha and Skyler and didn't even glance over at them. From the corner of his eye, he saw Skyler turn and stare at him, but he kept his head down trying not to look at her. If he did, Adrian knew he was going to either break down or cave in and go to her, and he couldn't let either thing happen. He had to do this. He had to give Skyler what she wanted, and that was a life without him.

* * * *

"Where's he going?" Skyler rushed into the house and up to Stefan who was still gawking outside with a frown on his face as if he was confused.

"I don't know."

Skyler noticed the funny expression on her brother's face, and it bothered her. "What do you mean you don't know? Weren't you just talking to him?" she snapped.

"Stefan, what's going on?" Natasha asked.

Stefan looked at Natasha, and Skyler suddenly got a funny feeling in her stomach, like what he was about to say wasn't going to be good. "I think that if Skyler didn't have his mark on her, Adrian would be rescinding his claim."

Natasha gasped and took a step backward, and Skyler could only stand there with her mouth open.

"Why in the world would he do that?" Natasha asked softly. "No male that I've ever heard of has dissolved a claim before."

"He's also been drinking and locked himself in his room through the entire heat." Dedrick came out of his office, newspaper in hand. "I know he suffered, but I didn't hear one sound out of him. He's broken."

"It's my fault?" Skyler asked, shocked.

Natasha shook her head no, but her brothers didn't say or do anything.

"No one said it was your fault," Natasha said.

"It's what you're all thinking." Skyler took a step back. "He was wrong!" Her voice shook and tears began to form in her eyes. "Stop making me feel as if it's all on me!"

Natasha quickly brought Skyler into her arms. "We are not trying to make you feel like it's all on you, honey. Boys, give us some time, please." Natasha led Skyler into her sitting room and over to the antique sofa where they sat down together.

"I don't understand," Skyler cried.

Natasha let Skyler out of her embrace and handed her a tissue. "Wipe those tears and then we're going to talk." Skyler did as she was told, and her mother smiled. "Now I thought you knew how our males were, so I'm going to take some of the blame for what's going on around here."

"What do you mean?" Skyler frowned and sniffed at the same time.

Natasha kept her smile in place and touched Skyler's face. "You never knew your father, and your brothers always kept their animal side hidden from you. I thought it was for the best, but now I see that it was wrong to do so. You should have known what our males can be like, both the good and the bad sides. Honey, you know the basics of when they go into heat, but not what they have to live with. Males need to find relief any way they can, and they do go to a willing female given the chance. It's hard for them to find their mates, and believe me when I say, once they do, they're treated golden. I know Adrian hurt you terribly when he went to your friend, and I really do believe that if he had known you were meant to be his, he never would have done that. I'm sure what he thought he felt then was his heat getting ready to come on, not his mate close by."

"But that doesn't change things." Skyler sighed. "He made a choice, and that choice was to sleep with my friend, and then put a claim on me." More tears slipped down her face. "He didn't even wash her scent off his body, Mom."

"Let me tell you a few things about your father. He was brought up in the old-fashioned way." Natasha dropped her hands onto her lap and took a deep breath as if she was recalling a memory that she wanted to forget. "He looked forward to the Gatherings in hope of discovering his mate and claiming her in the old way that his father would brag about. I guess if you wanted to say so, Drake was a true animal, but he never got his chance at the Gathering. And the old ways sometimes included a public mating."

Natasha shivered. "We stumbled upon each other at a different party that my father held to honor the mating of his best friend's daughter. Drake was there with his father. He was so dark and foreboding." Natasha smiled and chuckled, dropping her head for a few moments. "Dedrick looks so much like him. Anyway, the party was great, until your father saw me and in front of everyone demanded his rights as a male to lay claim on me. My father was furious, and his father proud. They boxed my father in a corner. See, back then, a male could lay claim and take in front of everyone, but my father didn't want that, and I was only eighteen."

"What did he do?" Skyler asked. It was the first time her mother had really told her anything like this before, so she was eager to hear anything about her father and how he claimed her mother. "How did he make Dad wait?"

"How he did it, I still don't know to this day, but my father was able to make Drake wait until I was twenty-one before taking me. I was so scared of him then, and the night of my twenty-first birthday, there he was on the doorstep. I was taken away from my home and family by this man I didn't really know.

"What I'm trying to tell you is this. Honey, Adrian could have taken you from your home and everything you've ever known, by his rights as a shifter male placing a claim, but he didn't. Adrian is an honorable male who is desperately trying to fix a wrong, and I know you're hurt over it, but you must also do the honorable thing and forgive him or at least work to get past it. Holding a grudge won't help either one of you, and it's already putting a tremendous strain on a relationship that hasn't even taken off yet."

"Didn't you hold a grudge over Dad taking you away?"

"If I was to have held a grudge over how your father had placed his claim, then who knows what would have happened, but once I got past the darkness that his father put in him, your father was my heart."

"How can I do either when he isn't around to talk to?" Skyler sniffed back the fresh batch of tears that she felt forming. "Why the hell does it even matter to me in the first place. He's only giving me what I want."

Natasha took a deep breath and brushed her hair with her hand. "Skyler, you are so much like me. I was just like you when I went home with your father. I fought him on everything, bitter over the way he claimed me." She took Skyler's chin and gently forced her to look her in the eyes. "Everybody makes mistakes. Don't let your mistake cost you your dream."

Chapter Six

Skyler waited patiently for Adrian to come back to the house. After she talked to her mother, she had thought it over and realized that she did need to talk to him. The only trouble now was that he wasn't around.

Day after day, he was gone until the days turned into a week and then another. He didn't call to let them know where he was, and with each passing day, Skyler began to fear that she had lost him for good.

Before she was ready to deal with it again, the full moon was coming, and that meant another cycle. Skyler had hoped that before this happened again, she would have her chance to talk with Adrian, but he continued to stay away. A few days before she was due to leave for the safe house, Skyler stood at her bedroom window looking up at the near-full moon when she heard his truck pull into the drive.

Skyler's heart began to pound, and her senses came alive with the simple knowledge that Adrian was home. She looked at the clock on her nightstand. It was a few minutes after midnight, and she was still dressed like she was going out for the night.

Biting her lip, she thought about what she should do. Sure, she needed to go and talk with him, but would he listen? Would he even let her in the same room? Skyler went over to the door, pressed her ear against it, and listened for him. She sensed Adrian when he moved quickly past her door.

Skyler waited a while before she left for his room. She thought he would probably take a shower before he did anything else. She gathered her courage while she waited until she thought enough time had passed. Opening the door, she took a deep breath. She figured this was her one and only chance, if she was to have her talk with him.

The house was quiet when she left her room. Everyone must either be sleeping or in their rooms, or doing whatever they felt like doing. Skyler thought about her brothers. She noticed that since she had talked with her mother, they seemed to act differently around her, too. She saw the disappointment in their eyes.

Skyler didn't knock when she reached his door. Instead, she turned the knob and walked inside. Right away, she smelled the lingering scent of the soap Adrian always used.

"Adrian," Skyler called out to him when she entered the dark room. She felt like a scared little girl waiting for the boogieman to jump out and get her.

"Not a good time, Skyler."

He sounded rough, and it scared her so that she jumped slightly. It took a few seconds for her eyes to adjust to the darkness and find him sitting on the floor with a towel around his waist, his legs drawn up and his arms and head resting on his knees.

"We…we need to talk," she stuttered, taking a step closer to him. She heard him struggle to breathe and frowned.

"No, we don't."

He sounded on edge. Skyler went over to him and knelt in front of him. She didn't touch him, mostly out of fear of him rejecting her touch. "Adrian, please."

She felt like the tables had turned suddenly. Now she was the one trying to pursue something here, and Adrian was fighting it. She reached out and touched his arm, and Adrian jumped back. He pressed against the wall fast and hard. He turned his head to the side in a way that made her think he was in some kind of pain from her touch. He emitted a low warning growl that had Skyler jumping back, but she ended up falling on her ass.

"I'm sorry," she whispered, tears coming to her eyes.

Skyler made to scoot back and leave but stopped when Adrian grabbed hold of her ankle tightly.

"I can't keep going back and forth." The pain was raw and evident. It sounded like he had been yelling for days. When he turned his head to look at her, Skyler saw pain deep in his eyes. He was almost broken, just like Dedrick had said he was. "I can't hang on the edge hoping that one day you'll forgive me and give me a chance."

"Trust is a hard thing to give out after it's been shattered," she told him and then took a deep breath. "I don't know if I can trust you with my heart."

Adrian moved to his knees and crawled to her slowly. She saw so much emotion in his blue eyes when he looked at her. "And I will swear on my life." He stopped when he was halfway up her body, and he lowered her down until she was lying back on her elbows. "That I will do whatever it takes to earn that trust again."

"And if it takes a long, long time?"

Adrian smiled. That smile had melted her heart when she was a teen. "Then I'll work a long, long time." He kissed her, a soft lingering kiss that held only tenderness.

"This isn't going to be easy," Skyler told him. She kept her eyes closed. Skyler felt as if she couldn't open them on her own. "I don't forgive easily."

He kissed her again, brushing his lips across hers. "I know," Adrian whispered. "I don't expect you to, either." Another kiss, this time he brushed her lips with the tip of his tongue and pressed her into the floor coming over her quickly.

Skyler loved kissing Adrian. The skill with which he moved his mouth over hers and the way he teased her with his tongue had her forgetting everything and focusing only on him.

She opened her mouth to him, sucking on his tongue as his body wedged between her legs. Adrian moaned and deepened the kiss. Skyler began to throb between her legs at the feel of his erection pressing against her core through the towel. It had always amazed her when she was young, and she had heard stories from the girls in school about how a kiss could have a girl burning for so much more. Now she had firsthand experience.

Adrian pulled away from her and rested his forehead against hers, his breathing coming quicker. "Why can't time be on our side?" he asked.

Skyler knew what he meant. The full moon was in a few days, which meant her cycle would be two days before that. Translation—she only had a couple days before her cycle began.

"You do know what happens on my cycle?" she asked, touching his face gently.

Adrian pulled back a little more and glanced down at her. "I know what's going to happen if you're close to me when your time comes."

With the way he was looking at her, Skyler couldn't breathe. Adrian pushed himself up and stood before her. He extended his hand to her. Skyler took it and let him help her up to her feet. She felt shaky. The heated gaze in his eyes made difficult the task of finding the words to answer his question. She didn't fight or protest when he moved her to the bed and lightly pushed her down so she was sitting on the edge.

"Your skin becomes very sensitive." He stood before her with his towel tenting from his erection. She wondered how the towel could stay around his waist with his cock standing straight out like that. "So sensitive that no one but me will be able to touch you."

He knelt between her legs and rubbed them slowly. When she relaxed and the tension left her legs, Adrian's hands moved up to the snap of her jeans. Skyler's mouth went dry.

"All you can think about is getting to me. You'll be dying to rub your body against mine, to fill the void you will feel between your legs with my cock."

He kept his eyes locked on her while he worked to keep her sitting and pull her jeans over her hips and down her legs where he stopped and worked on her shoes.

"You have felt it all before, when you went to the safe house, but this time, Skyler," he smiled, "this time, baby, it will be so much stronger." He finished taking her jeans off, then reached up to her shirt, and slowly pulled it up. "I don't want you to come to me still a virgin then, Skyler. We both will be in such need that slow and easy won't be a choice for us, and I don't want to hurt you." He finished pulling her shirt over her head so she sat in front of him in her bra and panties.

Rising to his knees, he kissed her deep and placed her arms over his shoulders. His arms came up, wrapping around her and unhooking her bra. Skyler felt herself falling back onto the bed when he moved, not once breaking his kiss. He slid her panties down her legs, then picked her up like a child, and moved her to the center of the bed while still kissing her.

When he did move his mouth from hers, it was to lower himself on top of her. Skyler moved her hands up in a feeble attempt to push him off. She still felt unsure about what was going to happen. She didn't think when she came in here to talk to him that it would lead to them having sex so fast. With her hands pressed between their bodies, and him wedged between her legs pressing his hot cock against her belly, Skyler felt the vulnerability and fear of a virgin. He was too close, too hot, and too much male all at once for her to handle.

"Adrian." Skyler knew she sounded scared, and she was. All of her instincts were screaming at her to fight, to get away, but the fear held her still.

His eyes changed to a deep red as he moved a hand between their bodies, touching Skyler between the legs. She arched into his hand, and her eyes drifted closed when he caressed her slit with his fingers. He teased her, touching her clit with the tip of his finger but never giving it the pressure it was quickly demanding. Her breathing hitched, and soon, Skyler felt her body come alive just as two of his fingers slowly pushed inside her.

There was no way she could stop the moan from slipping past her lips or the movement of her hips. Her legs parted more, and she dug her fingers into his chest as he moved with her, bumping her clit with this thumb.

In the blink of an eye, her climax hit. She cried out in pleasure and dug her nails harder into his chest. Skyler panted, forced to ride out the wave. Her hips bucked up to his fingers, and her clit quickly turned so sensitive that she thought she was going to scream.

"No more, please," she begged, tossing her head from side to side.

"We have so much more to do yet." He was so soothing that Skyler finally opened her eyes and looked at him. "I want you to try to relax." He kissed her deeply, plunging his tongue into her mouth to swipe against hers. "I'm not going to hurt you. I promise."

Skyler opened her mouth when he started to rub the tip of his cock against her swollen, wet labia. She squirmed more beneath him, causing his chest to brush against her pebble-hard nipples, which sent her nerves screaming for more. Skyler started to close her eyes, to let the sensations wash over her like a lover, but he didn't allow that.

"No." The velvety murmur caressed her. "Keep your eyes open. I want to see you, want you to watch me as I enter you for the first time."

He braced himself on his elbows and moved slightly so she could move her hands from between their bodies. Their eyes locked, and Skyler waited, but not for long.

She felt the scorching heat of his cock as he pushed inside her, parting her. Adrian was thick, and she wasn't sure if he would fit. Hell, Skyler began to wonder how anyone could do this. It wasn't pleasurable. In fact, it felt more like an invasion.

"Adrian...I don't think . . ."

Adrian cut her off. "Don't think, Skyler. I want you to feel."

"That's the problem." She moved her hands up to his chest, pushing. "It doesn't feel good."

He lowered his head and kissed her gently. "Trust me," he whispered. "It will soon."

She started to shake her head, but Adrian stopped the motion by kissing her deeply. His tongue thrust into her mouth, mating with hers, and this time she didn't try to stop the moan that escaped. This kiss was somehow different, deeper, with an edge to it, almost as if he were trying to eat her alive. Skyler kissed him back and moved her hands to his waist. Once she started to relax under him, Adrian slowly withdrew his cock, leaving the head, and then pushed back in short bursts of movement that matched the thrust of his tongue perfectly. It was enough to have Skyler wanting more.

She jerked under him when his finger touched her clit again. Skyler had been so absorbed in kissing Adrian that she never even felt him move his arm back between their bodies. Skyler moaned as he continued to touch her, and then spread her legs farther to encourage his touch.

As he played with the swollen nub, his mouth left hers to trail a heated path down her jaw to the shoulder that bore his mark. Not once did he stop the short, swift movements of his cock as it invaded her body. Skyler couldn't help thinking about how her skin felt during her cycle. She admitted it was very sensitive, but the things that Adrian did to her, the way he was kissing her had her skin feeling like it was on fire.

Stories she had heard in the past when listening at the door of Stefan's room—stories about what Adrian had done to other girls flew through her mind, but she couldn't recall him ever bragging about loving a girl slow and easy, like he was doing now. Her instincts were screaming that what he was doing now was all for her, that he had never treated another like he treated her.

"Oh God, Adrian!" Skyler cried as she arched her back and dug her nails into his sides. Another orgasm hit her from the skillful stimulation he gave her clit.

"Come on, come on, come on," Adrian whispered to her. "Ride it out."

Skyler opened her mouth to scream again, but he silenced her by kissing her hard and deep, thrusting his tongue into her mouth. At the same time, he thrust his cock to the hilt inside her body, tearing through her innocence. Her scream of pleasure turned into a gasp of pain, but the strangled cry was muffled by his kiss.

Skyler dug so hard into his sides that she felt blood trickle onto her fingers. She was thankful when he stopped moving and let her become accustomed to the invasion. Skyler was unable to stop the tears of both pain and intense emotions from slipping free.

"Shit, I'm sorry," Adrian groaned, resting his head on her shoulder. "We'll wait," he panted. "I'll wait a few minutes. Oh, man, I'm sorry."

Skyler gulped as much air into her lungs as she could and willed her body not to move. He had her under him, his scent consuming her, his mark branding her, and now Adrian had her innocence.

She wondered if it was over or if there was more. Deep down, if she were honest with herself, she knew it wasn't over. Her mother had told her a long time ago that if done right, both partners could get intense pleasure from mating. Right now, Skyler was having a hell of a time believing that. All she felt in that moment was pain.

"Adrian, I want to stop." Skyler's voice was strained, her fear coming out when she spoke.

He answered her with a lick to the mark he had made on her. The desire she felt rippling through her shocked her, and she began to throb where their bodies were connected. Skyler held her breath as he slowly pulled his cock from within her only to leave the thick head in place again. The breath she held shot out of her in a quick hard pant when he plunged back in sharply. Twice he did that before he stopped and rose up on his elbows to look down at her.

"Still want me to stop?" He grinned that sparkling grin Skyler had seen many times during the summers he had spent with them. Before she could answer, Adrian withdrew and then thrust back in. "Didn't think so."

He moved with purpose, speed, and with such tenderness that Skyler thought she was going to cry. He moved his hand down to cup her breast, brushing a thumb across the nipple before lowering it to her legs. Not once did he lose his rhythm. His cock moved in and out perfectly, touching spots inside Skyler that she had never known were there. The pleasure rose, chills raced down her spine, and finally, Skyler gave in—giving herself over to the pleasure that he gave her, climbing the ladder to the heaven she knew was awaiting her.

He moved his hand to rub up and down her leg while he kissed a scorching trail over her open mouth, jaw, neck, and shoulder. He even licked the sweat that had formed on her collarbone, and never did he slow down or miss a beat.

"Let it go," he whispered in her ear.

Skyler followed the motion of his cock, the grinding of his hips against her swollen clit. Skyler closed her eyes when she wrapped her legs around his hips and hooked one ankle over the other. She held onto him tight. The hard contours of his chest rubbed against her ultra-sensitive nipples. When the tidal wave of satisfaction she rode finally hit, Skyler went blind with the pleasure.

She screamed. Her body convulsed around his cock while he plunged inside her harder and faster. Skyler had heard and read that some women could feel their womb clench with the power of an orgasm, but had dismissed it as something from their imagination. Now she knew the truth. Her own womb convulsed with the power of her ecstasy, causing Skyler to wonder if it would hurt Adrian at all.

"Oh fuck!" Adrian cried. He braced both hands on the bed and, rearing up and back as far as he could go, shoving hard into her pussy.

Skyler felt his cock contract and spill his rich seed deep within her, and it seemed to trigger yet another orgasm from her. Skyler thought she was going to die. Getting air into her lungs was hard, and stars burst into joyous patterns behind her closed eyes—she'd never felt like this before.

Adrian dropped his weight on top of her, and Skyler welcomed it. Her legs and arms relaxed, and she soon felt limp. She was sure she wouldn't be able to move for weeks.

"Now I know." She sighed and let her eyes drift closed.

"Know what?" He shifted slightly, and Skyler sucked in a sharp breath at the ultra-sensitive feelings that hit her. He chuckled at her, removed his cock, and shifted his weight to the side but somehow managed to keep her under him.

Skyler smiled. "Now I know why Sidney has that goofy smile on her face all the time." With each word she spoke, Skyler drifted off into sleep, her smile still in place.

* * * *

Adrian watched Skyler sleep. Finally, he had her, and no one could take her away from him or dissolve the claim. She was his. His heart and soul, and if it took the rest of his life to right the wrong he'd done her, then he'd spend his life making it up to her.

He touched her forehead, brushing her hair off to the side before giving her a light kiss on her nose. Moving carefully, Adrian left the bed and padded naked, to the bathroom. Quickly, he cleaned himself up not only of his pleasure but also that of the blood that covered him—her virginity. An overwhelming sense of love and gratitude came over him. It was quite a gift that she had given him tonight.

When he came back to the house for a shower and change of clothes, he never dreamed that he would be making love to Skyler, or even coming to a small agreement to try to work past his mistake. Coming out of the bathroom, he smiled. Skyler had turned over in the bed and curled up into a ball as if cold. Adrian went over to her, cleaned her up the best he could, and then tucked a blanket around her before slipping into the bed next to her, giving her his warmth.

"You rest," he whispered, rubbing his face into her hair, taking in the sweet scent that was all hers, and wrapping his arms tightly around her. "From this time on, we start anew."

Chapter Seven

"Twins!" Skyler squealed to Sidney. "Are you sure?"

Skyler stood next to her bedroom window. She had been watching Adrian and Stefan play a one-on-one game of football in the backyard. In the morning, they had gone down to breakfast together, and Stefan seemed very happy to see Adrian back again. Her mother only winked at her, which said a lot. Dedrick, surprisingly, wasn't at breakfast, but when Skyler saw that Jaclyn was there, she didn't need to wonder why.

Skyler still had a few things that she and Adrian were going to need to work through, and she knew it was going to take some time, but in her heart, she hoped that with time all the wounds would be healed. Despite her glowing feeling, she knew trust would not come easily.

Looking at Sidney, who was beaming with the news, Skyler saw a different woman. She was still amazed at how her brother and Sidney had gone from kidnapping, bullying, and fighting with each other to being happy, in love, and about to have a family. Just watching her now gave Skyler hope that she would one day be at peace with Adrian in the same way.

"Oh, man." Jaclyn laughed, lying down across the foot of the bed. "You should have seen Stefan." She raised her head up to smile at Skyler. "I thought he was going to pass out again when he saw two in the sonogram picture."

"What did Mom say?" Skyler asked.

Sidney smiled. "Oh, not too much. She was just about as shocked as Stefan."

Skyler smiled and walked over to her bed. She sat down facing Sidney. She really was happy for her. "Well, it's very unusual. Our kind has found it very difficult to have children with humans, and for you to have twins, well, that is just...wow!"

"It also looks as if I am further along than what I thought, too,"

Sidney said, touching her belly. "I thought I was only about a month along. That's why I didn't tell anyone, and I knew about the difficulty of getting pregnant, but it seems I'm two months, almost three."

"And they're a very good size," Jaclyn put in. "So, he thinks she might have them early, which is normal when carrying two. So, I'm figuring." Jaclyn took Sidney's hand. "I should be done with my mother and back here in time for the birth."

Sidney sighed. She looked so happy, and the longing Skyler felt increased. She didn't have a close friend any longer. Once she had seen her so-called friend having sex with Adrian, the friendship had ended, and she didn't realize until that moment how alone she really was.

"Wish you didn't have to go." Sidney sighed again.

"Yeah, well look at it like this." Jaclyn smiled. "With me gone, Dedrick won't be such a bear." Lying back on the bed, she snorted and rolled her eyes. "I swear that guy has a corn cob up his ass when it comes to me."

Skyler couldn't help it and laughed. "No, he is like that every month." When Jaclyn glanced at her, she went on. "Full moon, remember? Dedrick has to go through his heat alone once again."

"Huh," was all Jaclyn said.

"So"—Sidney got Skyler's attention back on her—"I want you to help me with the nursery."

"Me?" Skyler was slightly taken aback. Since Sidney had been in the house and mated with Stefan, they really hadn't gotten that close to each other.

"Yes, you." Sidney laughed. "I don't want your mother to take over, and we need some time to get to know each other better, now that your brother is letting go some. I swear the whole time I've been here he has kept me all to himself."

"That's right," Jaclyn said, nodding. "You two are like sisters, so I'm putting you in charge of taking care of her while I'm gone." She looked around the room and then at Sidney, and clearing her throat, added, "Can I ask a question that has been nagging me since this morning?"

Skyler stood back up and went over to the window again. She caught herself staring once more at the two men who were playing like children. She faced Jaclyn and shrugged. "Sure."

Jaclyn sighed. "Okay." She sat up in the bed, crossing her legs in Indian style like Sidney. "Since you two came down together, and Adrian is now outside acting like he's ten, are you two like back to being a couple again?"

"Jaclyn!" Sidney cried in obvious shock. "That is none of your business."

"I'm just curious is all," Jaclyn said.

"It's okay." Skyler smiled. "I'm not really sure what we are." She frowned, staring back out the window. "I think you can call it a stalemate."

"How do you two put up with the alpha bullshit?" Jaclyn sighed, dropping back on the bed with her hands under her head. "I heard that Stefan kicked in a door once to get to Sidney. If you ask me, that's going a bit far to get your way."

"Tell me about it." Sidney laughed. "I thought Dedrick was going to pop a blood vessel in his neck, he was so pissed off at Stefan for that."

"I heard that my dad had all the locks on the doors taken off the first year they were mated," Skyler said, smiling as if she was lost in time. "He kept kicking in the doors to get to my mom."

"I can see that." Jaclyn smiled.

Skyler gave her full attention to the boys outside. Dedrick had joined the game, and Adrian threw the ball to him mere seconds before Stefan ran right into Adrian, knocking him down to the ground. The three of them were laughing and apparently having a great time. It almost seemed like the past month never happened at all. It was hard for her to believe that in such a short time, her life could change the way it had. The man she had a crush on for more years than she could remember was now here as her mate.

"Earth to Skyler," Jaclyn sang.

Skyler jumped and turned around quickly. "What?"

"What are you staring at?" Jaclyn scooted from the bed, went over to the window, and looked down at the guys. "Nice," she muttered.

Skyler knew that she was staring at Dedrick. It didn't take a magician to figure out that Jaclyn wanted Dedrick. Skyler wondered if he wanted her, too. Dedrick was a hard guy to get along with, and deep down, she was very glad Adrian wasn't like that. Skyler pitied the woman who mated with Dedrick.

"Sidney, how did you know that things between you and Stefan were going to be all right?" Skyler asked, leaving Jaclyn to stare out the window and going to sit on the bed.

Sidney shrugged. "I didn't at first. I wanted to choke your brother more than anything, and I hated him for taking me from my home and trying to force me to his way of thinking." Her eyes glazed over, and Skyler knew that she was remembering something. "I think when Mike threatened to kill him I discovered that everything he said was right. We did belong together, but that doesn't mean he always gets his way." She laughed.

Skyler smiled. "I guess you just needed time to get to know him."

"Some." Sidney nodded. "But are we really talking about Stefan and me or you and Adrian?"

"I'm afraid," Skyler said, tears threatening to spill over. All the raw emotion that overwhelmed her was driving her crazy. All she seemed to want to do was cry. "I don't think I can trust him."

"You won't know unless you try," Sidney told her. "Skyler, I've never dated, so I don't have much experience, but from what I've seen, he really is trying here." She shrugged again. "Maybe you should give him the benefit of the doubt."

"If he does his shit again, tell him you're going to cut his nuts off," Jaclyn said over her shoulder with a grin. Her eyes sparkled when she looked at Skyler. "The threat of neutering always brings them to heel."

Skyler laughed at Jaclyn and took a deep breath. "So when do we get to do the nursery thing?"

"Well." Sidney smiled slyly. "Stefan did say I can use the card again to get started since I'm further along than we thought and to have everything delivered. So whenever." She laughed. "I'm also going to need clothes."

Jaclyn turned back around and frowned. "How is Stefan going to deal with that heat crap with you being pregnant and the doctor saying you have to take it easy?"

"Oh, I can answer that one," Skyler spoke up. "Once the females are out of the first trimester, the males sort of calm down, like dormant with the heat. They still feel the need to mate, but it isn't that strong or demanding."

"Ah, so they go normal on us then," Jaclyn said. "'Bout time."

Sidney laughed. "I kind of like it when Stefan gets all animal on me." She blushed.

"Yeah, well, you don't know better." Jaclyn snorted, causing Sidney to laugh more.

Skyler went on. "It's more of an instinct thing. They sense how delicate their mates are, and their animal side just goes to sleep for about eleven months. Nine for the pregnancy, and two for her to recover."

"I have said it before, and I will say it again," Jaclyn retorted, turning back to the window. "You're all strange."

* * * *

Dinner that night turned into a cookout and pool party. Dedrick dressed in shorts, no shirt or shoes, and Stefan and Adrian were dressed in nothing but trunks. The three were playing a game of water basketball. Skyler sat at the side of the pool cheering Stefan on instead of Adrian. Sidney sat with Jaclyn in one of the lounge chairs, cheering Adrian on, and Natasha helped with the cooking. Every once in a while, Adrian would try to give Skyler a dirty look for cheering Stefan on, but his expression would fail, and then he'd splash her.

"I swear, Skyler." Adrian chuckled after Stefan managed to get past him with the ball. "Keep it up and I'm going to toss you in here."

Skyler laughed. "Yeah, and I'll just kick your ass worse than my brother," she said, taunting him. "Face it, Adrian, you suck!"

Adrian made a lunge backward for the ball, went underwater, and came back up right in front of her. "Is that so?" A grin spread on his face, and his eyes sparked with life.

"Yeah, that's so," she teased. Why was she flirting with and teasing Adrian? Skyler didn't know, but she did know that it felt good to be back to their old selves, back to what it was like when Adrian would come for summers and played water basketball.

Adrian took hold of Skyler by the waist and quickly dragged her into the water with him, never once losing his grin. "Let's make the game interesting then, shall we?"

Skyler took the ball from Stefan and waited until he was out of the water before facing Adrian. "And what did you have in mind?"

"Hmm, let me see." He swam around her and stopped behind her when he was really close. "I know," he said in her ear. "If I win, you have to give me a massage, um...in the nude."

Skyler turned to look at him. Her heart started to pound at the thought of being alone with him again, and her breath caught in her chest at his suggestion. "Are you out of your mind?" she whispered.

"Not confident enough?" He swam to the front of her.

"It isn't confidence I lack." She smiled. "I think you'll cheat."

"Yeah, you have to watch him, Sky," Stefan called out. Skyler turned to peer at her brother who was sitting down behind Sidney in the lounge chair with a plate full of food. "He does like to cheat."

"You're the one who cheats!" Adrian yelled to Stefan. He turned back, looked at Skyler, and raised an eyebrow. "Well?"

Skyler thought about it a few seconds longer before she grinned. "Okay, and if I win," she swam up close so only he would hear her, "you have to do the same thing, without the benefit of sex."

Stefan busted out laughing. "Shit, I heard that one!"

Skyler cocked her head to one side. "Are *you* confident enough?"

"Let's go," Adrian answered.

Skyler smiled, jumped up, and tossed the ball right into the basket. "That's one." She shrugged.

Adrian laughed. So did Stefan and Sidney. Also cheering Skyler on, Jaclyn moved to the side of the pool.

They moved around the pool fast, Adrian trying to keep the ball from Skyler, but Skyler managed to swim under him, steal it several times, and make baskets. Adrian also made a few, but not as many as she. Once, Adrian was trying to steal the ball and ended up grabbing a hold of Skyler, and it was called cheating by Stefan. It seemed the only one that was on Adrian's side was Dedrick.

Around the pool they swam, this time Skyler going after him for the ball, but Adrian managed to keep it out of her hands. "I only need this one last basket, and I win," she told him while smiling and laughed as he kept the ball fingertips away.

"That's why you're not going to get it," Adrian said. "I'm going to win!"

"Not on your life!" She laughed.

Skyler lunged for the ball, and Adrian wrapped his arm around her. Together, they went under, and in a flash, Adrian kissed her under the water. It was a quick kiss, one that was over by the time they surfaced, but it had Skyler's body coming alive again. She was so stunned by the time they came up, she couldn't stop him from making a basket.

"Now, I believe we're tied." Grinning, he swam to the side of her. "Your ball."

Skyler took the ball and watched him swim around the pool, smiling. "You really think you're going to win?"

Adrian grinned. "I have a very good chance."

"I'm calling the game!" Natasha yelled. "Dinner is ready, so why don't we call it a draw."

Adrian swam back over to Skyler and took the ball. "Saved by your mother," he whispered. Skyler turned, and with all her might, dunked Adrian by putting all her weight on his head, and then she swam quickly to the side of the pool. He sputtered as he gained the water's surface. "I'll get you for that, Skyler!"

Skyler laughed at him as she got out of the water. It felt good to relax, joke, and just enjoy family and friends, while not worrying about what was going to happen later, once they were alone again.

"I got it!" Jaclyn yelled.

Skyler wrapped a towel around her and went to help Jaclyn, who was helping to bring the food outside. Dedrick was grumbling something under his breath when she passed.

"I swear that brother of yours is driving me crazy," Jaclyn said to Skyler as she placed a tray of condiments on the table. "How the hell do any of you put up with him?"

Skyler laughed and helped Jaclyn set the table. "He usually stays out in the pool house when he's moody. It's the heat thing. Each month he's on edge, and we stay away from him."

"So if he is in a bad mood, why is he having dinner with us?" Jaclyn looked over her shoulder, and Skyler followed her stare. Dedrick was leaning against the house taking a long drink of his beer.

"Because we have company, and Mom told him he had to."

Jaclyn snorted. "Wouldn't bother me if he went and hid out." She turned back to Skyler and grinned. "Nice moves in the pool. I think you could have taken him."

"Not on her life!" Adrian snuck up behind Skyler and wrapped his arms tightly around her hips. He rested his chin on her shoulder. "I had the game totally in my hand."

Jaclyn cocked her head to the side and shoved a beer in his hand. "Yet, you still didn't win."

"Neither did she!" Adrian protested when Jaclyn turned her back on them and headed back into the house.

They all sat outside for dinner, eating grilled chicken, hamburgers, and sausages. Natasha fixed a large bowl of potato salad, and Jaclyn, at the last minute, fixed some homemade Mac-n-cheese, which Sidney informed everyone was her favorite.

The guys drank beer, and so did Jaclyn. Skyler started to feel like everything was slowly getting back to normal, or at least as much of normal as it could. Even though she and Adrian had come to some sort of an understanding, she still couldn't trust him.

Adrian didn't push for the contact that Skyler wasn't quite ready to give either. She knew from the way he would watch Stefan and Sidney, and then look at her, that he wanted to hold and touch her, too. When Skyler met his eyes, he grinned but didn't push, and that made her feel guilty. She wanted to give him what he was seeking, let him have that contact, but it came back to the trust thing. She knew that she should be over it, at least a little. After all, she did have sex with him last night.

By dark, Skyler felt exhausted. "Okay, I'm going to take a shower and go to bed," she said, pushing away from the table. She felt Adrian's stare at her back, but couldn't look at him. "Night."

* * * *

Sipping at his beer, Adrian watched Skyler leave. Tonight had been great. Skyler seemed to be her old self with all the teasing and playing around. He really hated for it all to end.

"I think I'm going to call it a night, too." Sidney yawned. "If you want a ride to the airport in the morning then you better get your ass in bed, too," she said to Jaclyn.

"Yes, Mom." Jaclyn rolled her eyes and laughed at Sidney.

"I'll be up in a bit." Stefan leaned over and kissed Sidney on the cheek.

"I'm going to turn in, too," Natasha stated. She smiled at the three of them. "I trust you boys will be able to handle cleanup?"

Adrian smiled and nodded when Stefan and Dedrick told her they would. He waited for the girls to leave, knowing that as soon as they were out of earshot, Stefan and Dedrick would start in on him. He wasn't disappointed.

"What's the story?" Dedrick demanded, sounding like he was pissed off about something.

"I don't have a story," Adrian answered.

"Bullshit," Dedrick growled. "You've been gone for almost a fucking month without a word. You tell Stefan that you would have relinquished your claim if you could, and now the two of you are all cozy again."

Adrian took a deep breath and let it out slowly, bringing his bottle up to his lips. "We're not cozy," he said before finishing off what was left in his bottle. "What the hell are you so pissed off about?"

"I'm pissed off because you take off and come back like nothing ever happened, so don't make me beat the answer out of you." Dedrick's eyes flashed red, and he sat forward in his chair and spoke in a lower tone. "Because it might give me intense pleasure and helps take the edge off of my fucking heat."

Adrian was a little taken aback over that. For Dedrick to be experiencing some early effects of his heat meant he was in worse shape than what any of them knew. "We're going to try to work things out," Adrian answered. "Happy now?"

Dedrick slumped in his chair. "No. I'm not happy."

"So you guys have talked then?" Stefan asked.

Adrian turned to him and nodded. "We're going to take it slow. I'm not going to try to bully her, and she's going to work at trusting me again." Dedrick grunted at that, so Adrian decided to turn the tables some. "What's the deal with you and Jaclyn? She shows up, and you become an instant prick."

"I'm going to kill her," Dedrick growled. "It's that simple."

Stefan chuckled. "The way it looks to me, the two of you are just itching for the other. How long has it been since you got laid?"

Adrian also laughed. "He has a point, Dedrick. The two of you are like a can of gasoline just waiting for the right match to come along and ignite you."

"Okay, first of all, we're not talking about me." Dedrick growled a warning. "We're talking about him." He pointed to Adrian. "Second, my getting laid is none of you dipshits business. Third, I can't stand her!"

"Uh-huh." Adrian smiled. "So what are you going to do now that the full moon is like three days away?"

"Why are you trying to change the subject?" Dedrick barked.

"Yeah, I'm noticing that too," Stefan remarked with a grin.

Adrian smiled and shook his head. "Look, we're not all over each other like Stefan is with Sidney, but we are coming to an understanding. I know Skyler doesn't want me to withdraw my claim, and I really don't want that either. So we're just going to take it slow."

"What about her cycle and moon night?" Stefan asked. "You've got a pretty good idea what she's going to be like then."

Adrian shrugged and looked up at the night sky. Three days left until he was in heat and less time for Skyler to go through her cycle. What he was going to have to do hurt him, but for any kind of relationship to form between them, he needed to do it. "I'm going to leave that up to her." He glanced back at Stefan. "If she wants to go to the safe house with your mother, I'm not going to stop her."

"Damn." Stefan sighed.

"Now that is what I call noble," Dedrick said, finally. "And, in my eyes, a male worthy of being in this family."

Adrian shrugged. "I'm not going to push." He finished his beer before glancing at Dedrick again. "If she still feels like she needs space, I'm going to give it to her."

"By giving up your rights as a mated male" Stefan whistled. "You have more willpower than what I would. No way in *hell* was I going to be kept from Sidney on moon night."

"I'm not giving up my rights." Adrian sighed. "Just taking things slow."

"I think slow is good." Dedrick nodded. "The house has been turned upside down, and I know I sure could use some peace."

Adrian raised his hands up in the air. "Peace, from what?"

Dedrick frowned. "From you two idiots!" He thumbed at Adrian and Stefan. "He drags Sidney here, and then there's your drama. You claim Skyler, and boom, more shit."

"Let's not forget about Jaclyn." Adrian smirked with his finger up in the air.

"She does bring out the best in my brother," Stefan said, teasing Dedrick.

"Not too bad to look at, either," Adrian added. Dedrick growled, and Adrian raised one eyebrow. "Oh, did my ears deceive me?"

"No, they didn't." Stefan leaned forward, his grin turning into a huge smile. "Is my brother interested?"

"Fuck off, both of you," Dedrick snapped. "I don't do humans, and stop changing the damn subject! We're talking about Adrian, not me."

"Ah, but you're so cute and huggable." Adrian got up from his chair, rushed Dedrick, and landed on his lap with his arms around his neck, hugging him. In falsetto, he said: "Come on, show me some love." Adrian puckered his lips and leaned in to plant a sloppy wet one on Dedrick's cheek.

"Get off me!" Dedrick growled.

"Come on, give some love," Adrian yelled.

Dedrick's chair tipped over backward. Stefan laughed as Adrian tried to pin Dedrick down. Adrian let out a sharp laugh and continued trying to kiss Dedrick, who only got more pissed. When he wrestled himself free, Dedrick rose and stormed off, leaving Stefan and Adrian doubled over in laughter in his wake.

* * * *

Skyler watched from her bedroom window as Dedrick and Adrian rolled around on the ground and Stefan sat in the chair laughing. She wasn't able to hear what they were talking about, but she could hear the laughter as they played around.

When Dedrick stormed off, mixed feelings came over her while she watched Adrian laugh like a little boy who'd just played a good trick on Dedrick. Skyler couldn't wrap her mind around her feelings for Adrian. She knew she needed to forgive him, but the fear of her heart being broken again paralyzed her.

"It's nice to see them getting along again." Natasha strolled up next to Skyler so silently that Skyler hadn't heard her. Natasha wrapped her arms around herself, smiling.

"They act like children." Skyler snorted.

Natasha laughed softly. "Honey, all men act like children. It's in their nature."

A few minutes went by while Skyler watched the horsing around below. "Mom, how were you able to stay with Dad when he bullied you?" Skyler turned to look at her mother, who was watching the guys below.

"There's an old saying you would do well to remember, Skyler." Natasha turned her head toward Skyler. "The bark is worse than the bite." She turned back to the window and chuckled. "Look." She pointed. "Stefan and Adrian got a hold of Dedrick when he returned to yell at them and were about to toss him into the pool." She shook her head. "I bet those three are going to be at it all night long."

"Mom?" Skyler waited, her arms crossed over her chest.

Natasha took a deep breath before turning toward her. "Everyone was scared of your father. I guess because he seemed so dark all the time, they assumed he was hard and cruel, but he wasn't."

Natasha took Skyler's hand, walked over to the bed, and sat down on the edge. "Honey, you're going to have to pick your battles and pick them carefully. Adrian is a proud male, and he should be, but you pushed him too hard."

"It sounds like your taking his side," Skyler mumbled.

"I'm not taking sides, Skyler. What I'm doing is pointing out a few things. You asked for space. He's given it to you. Now it's up to you to take the next step. Remember, I've been in your shoes and don't want to see your relationship turn sour before it even begins."

"I don't know how," Skyler whispered. "I don't know how to be a mate to him."

Natasha smiled and hugged Skyler. "Sure you do." She rubbed Skyler's back. "You've always loved Adrian. Now is your chance to embrace this opportunity, take the gift handed to you, and enjoy life to the fullest. He isn't expecting you to be something that you're not.

Adrian only wants you, and I think he has proved that."

Skyler nodded, and Natasha kissed her on the top of her head before standing up. "Now get some rest. Monday is around the corner, and we're going to be leaving for the safe house soon."

Skyler frowned. "You mean I'm not staying here?"

"Didn't Adrian tell you?" Natasha also frowned. "He told me this morning that you could go to the safe house instead of staying here if you wanted. I assumed you would want to go again."

Skyler stood and went over to the window. Her brothers and Adrian were all in the pool, playing around, trying to dunk each other and having a great time. Even Dedrick was smiling and seemed to be relaxed. It was something that was rarely seen.

"I'm not going," Skyler whispered.

"What? I didn't hear you."

Skyler turned to her mother. "I'm not going to the safe house. I'm going to stay here for my cycle and for his heat."

Raising her head, Natasha clasped her hands in front of her, and a small grin touched her lips. "You know what this means then?" Skyler nodded, so Natasha went on. "That's the first step, honey. No one ever said a relationship was easy, but I have faith that you and Adrian will be all right." She kissed Skyler on the forehead. "Good night, dear."

Skyler smiled and hung her head as her mother left her room. Then she looked out the window once more. Touching the cool glass, she felt a little overwhelmed. "God, I hope she's right."

Chapter Eight

Monday morning came and right when Skyler opened her eyes, she felt her cycle begin. Right before it hit, she tried to find Adrian to let him know that she was staying, but he seemed to always be gone or busy helping around the house. He was helping Stefan do work on the nursery and was often gone with Dedrick. When she would try to corner him to talk, one of her brothers ended up pulling him away from her. At night, when he came to bed, it was so late she was already asleep, and he was gone before she woke. If she didn't know better, Skyler would say that Adrian was keeping a distance between them, and she didn't understand why.

It also appeared that Thomas wasn't letting Skyler go as easily as the family had hoped for, and that was beginning to piss her off. If she had known he was going to get so possessive with a few dates, she would never have dated him. The last thing she needed was another man thinking she belonged to him, sort of like Adrian was doing. Then again, Adrian wasn't doing that, either, not when he was staying away from her.

A few hours after she had awakened, tingling, feather light sensations started on her skin as if someone was grazing the tips of their fingers all over her, and it had her skin crawling. The sensations had Skyler feeling as though she needed to rub against something hot and hard, and that made her think of Adrian. She hated how it felt, and hated it even more when she tried to get dressed. Everything she wore felt like sandpaper next to her skin, and this month seemed worse than any other, all because she had had sex with Adrian. A change had been started, one that caused her cycle to be stronger and her body a hell of a lot more sensitive than she could ever have imagined.

Skyler tried to take a shower, and almost screamed when the water touched her. Her breasts felt heavy and swollen. When she touched her nipples, she almost cried out from not only the sensitivity but also from pain. Skyler was starting to hurt from the arousal slowly building in her body. A bath made it somewhat better, but not much. Soon the warm water of the bath became more of a torture for her clit than anything else. By noon, she was on fire from the inside out.

Every nerve was alive and screaming, and, she could feel them all. Her pussy grew wet, and the folds of her labia were swollen and thick. Her clit throbbed in an almost agonizing need, and for the first time ever, she thought she could feel her womb contract.

Everything was new to her, and all she could really focus on was what Adrian had told her. He had said that her cycle would be painful this time and that her body would want to seek out her mate. Skyler knew that Adrian wasn't going to come to her. He was giving her the space she needed in order to come to terms with this claiming. It had also occurred to her that he didn't know she stayed home instead of going to the safe house. Skyler had never gotten the chance to talk to him at all. So, if Skyler wanted relief, she was going to have to go to him for it.

By five, she had had enough. Skyler winced as she put on her silk robe and her skin seemed to scream in protest from the touch of the fabric. She whimpered with each step she took. She felt like she weighed a ton, and her clit throbbed with each step. Lucky for Skyler, Adrian's room was not too far down the hall from hers.

While she walked, she prayed that he would be in his room and not helping Stefan again or doing some stupid shit with Dedrick. She needed him, and although she hated it and tried to tell herself it would pass, she knew that this time it wouldn't.

She needed Adrian to help her get through this, the same he was going to need her to help him in a couple of days. Skyler couldn't get over how miserable she felt, and it all had to do with her now being mated.

"Please be here," she whispered, struggling to stay upright and open the door.

Skyler almost dropped to the ground and sobbed her relief when she heard the shower running in the bathroom. Adrian was here. As soon as she closed the bedroom door, the water stopped. Moments later, Adrian came out of the bathroom. Water dripped from his body, and he held a towel around his waist.

"Skyler?" He frowned. "What's wrong? Why are you here? You should be at the safe house."

"You were right." She shook and found that talking was close to impossible. "It hurts worse than anything." She shook her head when he frowned at her. "I couldn't go…not this time."

Adrian didn't move. She thought she saw some disbelief in his eyes. *He must not know what to do or he'd be making an advance.* Skyler was going to have to go all the way she realized. She forced her legs to move, bringing her closer to his dripping body. While she walked, she pulled at the tie of her robe. By the time she reached him, she had it open and sliding down her arms. Soon, she stood naked before him.

Just standing close, feeling the warmth of his body seemed to calm the raging need that built to a point that her hands were shaking. She was scared to reach out and touch him.

"I don't want to fight anymore," she told him and followed him as he took first one and then another step back. "I don't want to hurt," she continued as he took several more steps away from her. When his back touched the wall, he stopped. "And you have to promise me that after tonight, we start anew." She swallowed hard, looking him up and down. "That you will never hurt me like that again," she whispered. "I'll die if you do."

With one hand flat on the wall, the other holding his towel around his waist, he swallowed hard. "I swear on my life, Skyler," he rasped. "I'll never hurt you like that again."

The heat she felt from his body was only doing so much to ease her. The desire within was building. Skyler wanted to fuck, and she wanted it now! "I…I…" She took a deep breath and let it out slowly.

"It's okay," Adrian told her softly. "Just do what you feel is right. Take from me whatever it is you need. I'm here for you."

Skyler nodded and licked her lips. Her hands shook with her need as she brought them up and touched his chest lightly. He was a hot, muscular male, and he felt so damn good underneath her hands. Skyler leaned in close, putting her face mere inches from his chest and took his male scent deep into her lungs.

Adrian was clean, freshly showered, but Skyler could smell his own heat about to start. After this night, as they would both rested after her cycle, which would last a full twenty-four hours, like the male's heat, then Adrian's heat would start to build. Twelve hours would be all the rest they would get before they next came into their need, and Skyler could already smell it. Within those three days, Skyler could conceive, so she would either be pregnant or bleed. It was that simple.

"I can smell it," Skyler whispered. She pressed her cheek against his chest and both hands flat on his stomach. "Your heat is near."

"Don't worry about my heat." His voice rumbled gently as he spoke.

She moved her head from his chest with a nod but didn't glance up at him. Skyler slid her hands to the towel around his waist. With a hard yank, she took it away from him, looking her fill at his cock, which was swelling before her eyes.

She closed her hand around the base, and Adrian sucked in his breath. Skyler glanced up at him fast, thinking that she might have hurt him, but the expression on his face was anything but pain. His eyes were closed, his mouth open, and his breathing was coming quickly. Skyler also heard a faint "'Motherfucker" slip past his lips.

"Like this?" she asked, moving her hand up then down to the base of the shaft. His only answer was a nod. Keeping her eyes on the rise and fall of his chest, Skyler picked up the pace. "I want to taste you."

"Oh shit," Adrian whispered. "Skyler, I'm not sure..."

She didn't give him the chance to finish whatever he had been about to say. Skyler dropped to her knees, and like a starved animal, she took his cock deep into her mouth. Skyler knew that she didn't have the skill he was used to, and she hoped she was doing it right. At the same time, she didn't really care. Skyler was thinking about herself right now, and she had to taste him or die.

Skyler sucked on him greedily, pulling at the flesh and flicking her tongue over every part she could. She loved how he moaned and how his hips thrust against her.

"Shit, Skyler." Adrian moaned. "If you don't stop...oh, hell!"

He came, and Skyler nearly lost control. He tasted wild, spicy in her mouth, causing her to want even more. Although she hated to, Skyler released him and stood. Adrian was breathing hard, his eyes closed, and Skyler thought it was one of the most beautiful sights she had ever seen.

He was against the wall, his cock still hard and his eyes closed.

"Can you do more?" Skyler asked curiously.

Adrian opened his eyes and grinned at her. "Oh, yeah."

He picked her up as if she weighed nothing. Skyler wrapped her legs around his hips, moaning softly when his cock bumped against her swollen mound. She was so sensitive between her legs, and so ready for him to enter her that she knew she wouldn't last once they got started.

"Adrian, I can't wait." Skyler moaned, rested her head on his shoulder, and tried to wiggle her body closer.

"Then, you won't have to," he told her, swinging around and pushing her up against the nearest wall.

Skyler cried out when she was impaled hard with his cock. Adrian stretched her to the max, and it felt damn good. He pounded into her hard, slammed her against the wall, and still, Skyler begged for more. She needed the roughness of the act, just like he was going to need it with her. The only difference right now was that Adrian was starting it, but before this night was over Skyler was going to have him under her, doing exactly what she wanted.

"Harder," she whimpered. "Please, Adrian, I burn."

Adrian moved hard, almost brutally, causing Skyler to scream. She shattered around him. Star blinding pleasure hit, and Skyler did all she could to hang on to him and ride out the wave.

"We can't do this here," Adrian said, breathing hard. "We can't go through your cycle against the wall."

"Take me to the bed." Skyler gulped air into her lungs.

When he moved, his cock still embedded in her body, she whimpered again. Her whole body was sensitive, and with his strides to the bed, she was going to come all over again.

Doing as she asked, he laid her on the bed under him, but Skyler was having nothing to do with that. Quickly, and with her own strength, which was increased tonight, Skyler flipped him onto his back. She didn't waste time lowering herself onto his cock. Skyler braced her hands on his chest. She closed her eyes, moving her hips and taking what she needed to get through this period.

She rode him hard. The bed moved with her, and Adrian moved his hands from her waist and cupped her breasts, squeezing the mounds while bucking under her. She moaned, the pleasure gripping her in a spell that she wasn't sure she was going to be able to get out of.

"Yes." Adrian moaned. "Oh, shit, Skyler. Baby, oh fuck!" He moaned louder, and when Skyler opened her eyes and looked down at him, she saw his eyes were closed and his head was pushed back into the softness of the mattress. "Yeah!" He moaned.

Skyler gave into her feelings and did the one thing she knew she would never be able to take back or deny the next time they got into a fight. The moment she felt her orgasm come, the one that she knew was going to be the best, she leaned down and bit Adrian hard on his chest, right above his left nipple. He cried out and wrapped his arms tightly around her. Sucking at his chest, she tasted blood from her bite but found that she couldn't let go, not when she felt Adrian throbbing inside her. His climax matched her own in power and strength.

While she hung on to him with both her arms and her mouth, Skyler waited for the burning to ease, and it did after a few tender moments. Adrian rubbed her back while she eased in his arms, licking at the wound she left.

"Feel better?" Adrian asked softly.

Skyler stopped messing with the mark and rested her head under his jaw. "I'm tired." She sighed, snuggling closer. "But I still feel hot."

"Then how about we take a bath to cool you off a little?" He stood, and Skyler cried out from her sensitivity.

He carried her into the bathroom, which was not as large as hers. All of the guest rooms were a nice size, with the old-fashioned tiger claw bathtubs that could hold two. He sat her down on a stool and began running the water for a cool bath. Skyler couldn't seem to look him in the eye as they waited. She felt slightly ashamed at how she had fucked him on the bed and then bit him. The bite appeared like it was bruising when she dared to take a glance up. Not once did she ever think that during her cycle she would have Adrian here and that she would practically attack him. And the biting thing? Where the hell did had that come from? Skyler knew that males bit and left marks, but hadn't thought she would have the urge to do it. Everything going on was too much at once for her. Too many emotions, thoughts, and brand new instincts were hitting at once, and Skyler was pretty sure it all had to do with her cycle.

"You know you don't have to be embarrassed with me," Adrian said, breaking the uncomfortable silence. "I'm not going to hold this over your head."

He helped her get up and into the tub as it filled. Skyler was a little surprised when he stepped in behind her, sat, and pulled her onto his lap, wrapping his arms around her. As much as she tried to fight, she couldn't, and she relaxed against him.

"Man, that feels good." Sighing, she closed her eyes and enjoyed the way he was rubbing her arms and shoulders.

"You're relaxing," he said in her ear. "That's good."

Skyler opened her eyes but didn't move. "I'm sorry, Adrian," she whispered. "I didn't mean to come in here and use you like this."

"Don't be." He moved his hands up to her neck and began to rub out the knots. "I told you I would be here for you when you need me."

Skyler sat up and turned. She braced her weight on her hands between his legs in the water and leveled her face with his. "No, I'm sorry for the way I've been acting. Sorry for trying to shut you out."

He touched her cheek, brushing some wet hair behind her ear. "Don't be sorry. I should be the one at your feet begging for forgiveness every day." He grinned then. "I deserved it all for what I did. I'm the one that needs to say sorry to you every day of my life."

Skyler moved up his body and kissed him deeply. For first time ever, she had taken the initiative and kissed Adrian. The other times, he had kissed her, but this time, it was all her. "Oh, and I'm sorry about that," she whispered against his lips while brushing a finger over his wound and grinning when she felt his cock harden again under her.

"Oh, I'm not." He smiled, wrapped his arms around her waist, and brought her closer to him. "I loved it."

Skyler smiled and kissed him again. "I think it is going to leave a mark."

Adrian started kissing her neck, while he moved his hands down to cup the globes of her ass. "Um, I don't mind."

Skyler moved over him and slowly lowered herself onto him. Adrian moaned.

"Oh fuck, Skyler. You feel so damn good."

"I need more," she whispered, moving her hips slowly, which caused tiny waves in the bathwater.

"You take all you want, baby." Tightening his grip on her ass, he helped her to move. "I'll give you anything you want."

Skyler fucked Adrian as hard as she could in the tub. Water splashed onto the floor; moans echoed off the walls, and tongues played a mating game all their own. They spent almost an hour in that tub loving each other. Once Skyler was finally spent, her orgasm rushing through her so hard she almost passed out from it, she rested.

Breathing hard, she laid her head on his chest and enjoyed the short aftershocks of her pleasure as well as his. Adrian held her tightly, cocooning her in his arms, making Skyler feel safe and protected. When she started to shake from the cool water, Adrian drained the tub and stood up, holding Skyler as though she was a child.

Skyler didn't mind when he dried her and dressed her in one of his shirts, then tucked her into his bed. She smiled at him and welcomed his warmth when he slipped under the covers with her. Her cycle, like his heat, would slowly disappear, leaving Skyler drained. She would sleep hard, and most likely, she would sleep for half of the next day. Then she would awaken refreshed for his heat cycle. After it was over, they would wait for a couple of days to see if she was pregnant or if she would start to bleed. Skyler sighed, content for the moment. There was nothing she could do now but sleep so she could get the rest she needed for when Adrian started his heat.

Skyler was drifting off to sleep, her head resting on his chest, his heart beating steady in her ear. She thought about telling him something that she had kept close to her heart for so long. Thought about what he might say upon hearing it, but her exhausted body had other plans. So before she could let the three simple words "I love you" slip past her lips she fell asleep.

* * * *

Adrian dragged his sorry ass into the kitchen around ten that night. He was tired and surprisingly sore in a few places, especially on his chest where she'd bit him. Skyler had been sleeping for hours, which was good for her. She was going to need her rest for tomorrow night. She was also going to have to wake up and eat something. Skyler might have been needy and on edge, but once Adrian's heat started, he would become damn demanding of her whether he wanted to or not.

"I was wondering if I was going to see you today or tonight."

Adrian jumped when Dedrick spoke from his place at the small kitchen table where he sat drinking a beer, looking worn out.

"Thought I would fix something to eat for Skyler," Adrian said. He started to turn to the fridge, but stopped. "What's up?"

"Just chilling out with a cold one." Dedrick shrugged before bringing the bottle up to his lips and draining what was left. "Want one?"

Adrian frowned. "Sure." He sat down across from Dedrick and took the beer. "You're not acting like yourself." He twisted the cap and tossed it into the trash can before taking a long drink. "Why?"

"Guess I've been thinking about something you said," Dedrick answered. He also twisted the cap from another beer and took a drink.

"You mean what I said about Jaclyn?" Adrian asked. He was afraid that Dedrick would explode on him.

"Yeah." Dedrick sighed. "I don't understand what's going on. I feel strange when she comes for her visits, and I'm starting to think it isn't very safe for her to be around me."

"Yeah, well, I can't see Jaclyn taking any kind of warnings too seriously." Adrian shrugged. "I don't know her that well, but I do get the vibe that she's the kind of woman who goes after what she wants. I think she's the kind of woman that would be well pursued if she were a shifter female."

"That's another thing," Dedrick growled. "I have no interest in human women. Never have in my whole life, but with her." He shook his head. "I don't fucking know."

Adrian couldn't stand it any longer. "What's really going on here, Dedrick? What aren't you telling me?"

Dedrick rubbed his face and, it was then that Adrian saw the battle his friend was fighting. The heat wasn't going well for Dedrick. He needed to find his mate, and he needed to do it soon before it became dangerous for everyone around him.

"I don't know, man." The sigh that came out of him was enough for Adrian to see how worn down Dedrick really was. "She's my sister-in-law's best friend, almost like family, but lately when she makes those teasing remarks about getting laid or nitpicks, it isn't pissing me off like it should."

Dedrick glanced at Adrian, and Adrian saw it all. Dedrick wasn't only having a major battle going on with his heat, but a battle with something deeper. "Are you trying to tell me…?"

Dedrick took a deep breath, sat up in his chair, and leaned forward. "I don't get this, Adrian. I can control myself just fine, but when I get around her, I feel almost primal. I can't decide if I want to choke the shit out of her or fuck her until she can't talk from screaming so much."

Adrian chucked. "That is a problem."

"If Sidney finds out, can we say castration?" he groaned.

"I think you're blowing this all way out of proportion," Adrian said after a few minutes. "There's just a lot of shit going on in the house. There's an unclaimed female among us, and your heat is close, so I think you're just looking at her like an outlet is all. Hell, I almost feel sorry for you." Dedrick gave him a dirty look, so Adrian went on quickly. "Just for the fact that you have to watch Stefan and Skyler being mated is all." Laughing, Adrian brought his beer up to his lips. "I would hate having to go through what you are about to alone…again.

"Yeah, well, it isn't a fucking picnic," Dedrick grumbled. "Would love to be in Stefan's shoes right now and have it all go dormant."

Adrian stood and went to the fridge. He worked fast at putting together something to eat for Skyler. "Your time will come, man."

Adrian put some leftovers on a tray and heated it up for Skyler and a meatloaf sandwich on a tray for himself before he took another beer. He glanced back at Dedrick as he picked up the tray. "There is someone out there for you, Dedrick. You're just going to have to open your eyes a little wider to find her."

Dedrick snorted, sat back in his chair, and stretched his legs out in front of him, crossing them at the ankles. "Shut up and go back to your mate."

Adrian smiled. "Don't have to tell me twice."

Chapter Nine

Adrian was alone when he woke around noon. He was facedown with his arms and legs stretched wide, blankets barely covering his bare ass. He was dead tired. His chest throbbed where Skyler bit him again. After he woke her up to feed her, she pushed him back onto the mattress and rode him hard, finishing off with her teeth under his right pec.

Groaning, he pushed himself onto his back and looked down at the many marks she had made. Only one stood out from the rest and would be permanent, the others would fade away in a few days. Adrian smiled and touched it gently. The spot was tender and bruised, just like he knew hers was going to be tonight.

Adrian dragged his sorry butt out of bed and headed to the bathroom. His muscles protested each step he took, and he rolled not only his shoulders but also his head to try to loosen up as much as he could. While he started the shower, Adrian wondered how Skyler was doing. He knew that if he was achy, she had to be even worse, because of the many times they had come together.

He stood under the hot spray, letting the water cascade down his neck to travel over his back and legs. It felt good and helped to relax him, but what it didn't do was help with the heat that was slowly starting to plague him. By tonight, he would be in full-blown need, taking Skyler hard, just as she had tried to take him.

After his shower, Adrian found a pair of sweatpants and a plain white T-shirt. He didn't see the point in bothering with shoes, so he left his feet bare. When he left his room, he noticed right off that the house was very quiet, more so than usual.

No one was in the dining room, but Stefan was in the kitchen reading the paper with a huge sandwich in front of him.

"Hey," Adrian greeted him, looking around. "Where's everyone at?"

Stefan put the paper down and pushed the sandwich toward Adrian with a grin. "Mom took Sidney shopping for paint. Dedrick is in the pool house, and Skyler is upstairs in her room taking a nap."

Adrian picked up the sandwich and took a large bite. He closed his eyes and sighed while chewing it. Food always tasted great to him after sex or a great night of sleep, and this time, it tasted better than ever. "Damn that's good."

Stefan laughed. "You're a strange man."

"Never claimed to be normal."

Stefan snorted and then grinned. "So, she's okay?"

Adrian wiped his mouth with a paper napkin and nodded. "She's fine…wore my ass out." He grinned.

"Don't give me the details of my sister's sex life, please." Stefan wrinkled his nose, but his grin was still in place. "Mom called to check in. She was pretty worried about her. Told me that Skyler decided to stay instead of going to the safe house and asked me to keep an eye on her."

Adrian met Stefan's gaze. "I think we're going to be okay now." A few minutes went by before he smiled at Stefan. "So how are you going to handle tonight, with Sidney?"

"Now that is private." Stefan tried to act offended, but it didn't work. "I'm okay. Don't really feel it starting, you know? Almost feels as if it's not there."

"Dedrick wishes he could feel like that," Adrian said and took another bite of his sandwich. "I'm starting to wonder about him."

"You're not the only one." Stefan sighed. "I'm worried about him, and so is Mom."

"Do you think there's something going on between him and Jaclyn?"

Stefan groaned, rubbing his face and then the back of his neck. "I hope not. Dedrick doesn't do well when it comes to fooling around with humans. Years ago, he messed around with one and got very rough with her. She claimed she liked the rough stuff, but apparently not the way Dedrick played. He almost hurt her real bad, and since then, he stays away from humans when it comes to sex. I keep telling Jaclyn to stay away from him. Even Sidney has told her to tread lightly, but I don't think she's listening."

"I don't think treading lightly is her way." Adrian grinned. "I think he's interested, and I *know* she is."

"Then keep your fingers crossed that he doesn't act on it," Stefan said, all humor gone from his eyes. "If they hook up, Jaclyn is going to get hurt. Dedrick isn't the type to commit."

"He needs his mate. If that mate turns out to be a human, he needs to be able to come to terms with it. We don't always get what we expect. Mother Nature can be a bitch, and my gut tells me that we are in for one hell of a show when it comes to your brother." Sitting back in his chair, Adrian crossed his arms over his chest. "Jaclyn strikes me as the kind of woman who goes after what she wants and damn the consequences. She wants Dedrick, Stefan. I would bet everything I have on it."

Stefan took a deep breath and let it out slowly. "Well, let's worry about tonight first. Sidney said Jaclyn should be back around the time the babies are born, so we've got time to figure out this mess."

Adrian chuckled. "Not my mess. I have my hands very full with your sister, and I plan on keeping it that way." He stood up, shoving the rest of the sandwich into his mouth. "I've learned my lesson," he said with his mouth full.

* * * *

Skyler spent the whole day resting, and Adrian spent it in his room pacing. He watched the clock and the sun, waiting for time to go by and dealing with the heat slowly building with each passing minute. Adrian had his time frame down like a woman who was keeping track of her cycle each month. He knew the exact time that he would be in full-blown heat.

At four in the afternoon, his body started to itch for Skyler. The pain also came, but it wasn't as bad as the misery he felt in his skin. He needed to be in the same space as Skyler, smell the scent, and feel the warmth of her body. Adrian had only one hour to go before he was in raging heat, so he left his room to go to Skyler's.

Adrian walked inside quietly and took a deep breath of Skyler's scent, at once feeling both calmness and a desperate need for her. He heard her in the shower, saw the bed was fresh and turned down, and he knew that she was waiting for him, preparing her room for his heat and what he might need.

Adrian closed and locked the door. He pulled his shirt over his head and slid the sweatpants down. Naked and hard as stone, he waited for the water to turn off and his mate to step into the room with him. She came out, and Adrian felt his mouth go dry. His cock throbbed with newfound life. Raw, unquenched hunger mixed with lust hit Adrian so hard he thought he was going fall over from it.

"You okay?" he asked, not recognizing the roughness in his voice.

Skyler gave him a shy grin before dropping the towel at her feet. "I'm fine," she told him so seductively he could almost feel it caressing his skin. "And still tired."

Adrian growled. He couldn't stop the sound from coming forth. "Well, you're going to drop when I'm done with you."

He could smell her desire and knew she was wet and ready for him. Adrian went up to her, took her by the arms, and brought her body close, kissing her deeply. As fast as the kiss began, it was over, and he was tugging her to the floor, flipping her over to her hands and knees. With his heat racing in his system like a drug, Adrian felt like he was on the edge of a cliff and the only way back was Skyler.

His conscious self wanted to go slow and enjoy this time with her, to relish finally having a mate during his heat, but the beast inside wasn't having it. He wanted to claim, to conquer, and to take, and Skyler was his by all rights of the shifter male race. There was little to nothing in foreplay, and tonight, Adrian didn't feel like he had the time to waste with it.

He thrust into her with everything he had. Crying out, Skyler pushed back against him, which drove Adrian crazy. She was so tight, so damn hot and wet that he felt as if he was going to burst into flames just by being deep inside her.

"Don't stop," Skyler begged, while wiggling her ass and grinding him deep inside her.

Adrian answered her with a growl. He took hold of her hips, holding her in place and moved. His hips slapped into her ass, driving his cock as fast and as hard as he could into her. With each movement, he felt as if it wasn't enough, that he wasn't getting the right friction or hitting the right spots for her.

"Oh God, yes, yes, yes," Skyler cried. She pushed back against him and climaxed

Adrian kept pounding within her, forcing Skyler to ride one orgasm after another until she was screaming at him to stop for a few moments. Surprisingly, Adrian still hadn't come yet. He thought most of that had to do with what Skyler had done to him the night before.

Adrian stopped and growled a warning when she crawled away from him. He sat back on his heels, his cock standing out in front of him, glistening with her juices. He watched her move farther and farther away. His instincts were screaming for him to charge her and fuck her again, but he fought it. Skyler was playing with him. He saw it, and he loved it.

"Your eyes are bright red," Skyler said, turning onto her back to rest on her elbows, giving Adrian one of the best views in his life. "Do you feel the burn?"

He heard the teasing tone of her words and said, "Why don't you come back over here and feel it with me?"

His gaze never left her body as she rose to her feet. "Why don't you make me?"

Adrian smiled and stood slowly. It was a challenge any shifter male would not be able to resist. "With pleasure," he rumbled with a growl and narrowed his eyes on her.

Rubbing her breasts and teasing him, Skyler backed away from him. Adrian lunged and missed her by inches. She laughed and ran from him to the far side of the room, putting the bed between them. Adrian jumped onto the bed. He growled and moved to the center of it so she would know without a doubt that if she moved, he would have her. Skyler backed into the corner of the room, and like a beast corners its prey, Adrian stalked toward her.

"Change, Adrian," Skyler whispered. "Let it all out."

Adrian jumped from the bed and stood in front of her. He could smell her rising desire. It matched his own. Adrian stood before her and changed. His frame increased, and sandy brown hair began to sprout all over his skin. His bones popped and reformed into an almost different body. His hands and feet changed into large paws, and his face took on the appearance of a wolf with a thick neck, snout, and sharp teeth. There he stood before Skyler, not as a man but as the beast that Adrian and other shifter males were on the inside; the animal that only Skyler could now control.

Licking her lips, Skyler smiled. "Now." She rubbed her arms, and Adrian picked up her desire. It changed in scent, becoming darker, muskier, thicker, and so much richer. "Finish it."

Adrian closed the distance between them and lifted Skyler into his arms. He tossed her onto the bed, turning her so that she lay on her side, and then he crawled onto the bed, placing his body between her legs. His face changed back to normal, hair reseeded, but the thickness of his body didn't. Taking hold of one leg, moving it high in the air for what he wanted, he shoved all nine inches of his thick cock back inside until his balls touched her ass.

"Shit, Adrian." Skyler moaned, rotating her hips as much as she could.

Adrian took her hand and placed it between her legs. "Rub." His command was deep and thick, sounding like a cross between a man and a beast.

Skyler did as he ordered, and Adrian moved with extra force. He pounded into Skyler, rocking the bed with each hard thrust. He felt it, the strong pull of his beast to claim, to mark. Adrian was almost there, almost to the end but not quite. One big orgasm and the burning need would slowly subside, and his animal side would calm.

Adrian had always been different when it came to his heat. Some of the males could orgasm over and over again during their time, but Adrian only did once. Sure, he could fuck hard and long, giving his partner many orgasms in a row, but for him to get that completion meant the end of his cycle. He felt that end coming.

He growled as he moved, and Skyler whimpered. He felt her body tighten when his own orgasm rushed down his spine to his heavy scrotum, and Adrian turned her so she was on her back. He grabbed her wrists, pinning them over her head as he lowered his body to hers.

Adrian reared back and howled. His cock erupted, pouring not only his seed into her body but also the need and burn of his heat. Collapsing onto her, he closed his mouth over the mark and bit down as he waited for his body to come down from its high, enjoying the aftershocks.

As he fought to catch his breath, his body slowly changed back to its normal state. Skyler wrapped her arms and legs around him. In all his years, Adrian never thought that having a mate during his heat would feel this good. To have the release, to be held in her arms while he calmed was worth the wait and all the fighting.

It took a few minutes before Adrian felt strong enough to pull away from her. He groaned when his now-limp cock slipped free from her warmth. His cock was so sensitive he could barely stand it. With a tug, Adrian pulled Skyler to her feet, and together, they went into the bathroom for a quick shower. Even though it felt like it had lasted ten minutes, the clock on the stand read midnight, and they had started around ten that night. His heat and her cycle were over. Adrian felt like he was about to drop, but he still managed to pick Skyler up and carry her out of the bathroom and to the bed.

In the bed, they lay together, Skyler resting her head on his chest and draping one leg over his waist. Adrian had his arm hooked tightly around her, his chin resting on top of her head. He was so relaxed he felt as if he could sleep for a week.

Peace. That was what Adrian felt having Skyler in his arms. He felt calm, and he didn't want to let it go—ever.

His eyes slowly began to drift closed, and sleep almost had him when Skyler broke the silence. "Adrian."

"Hum?" Hugging her close, he kept his eyes closed.

"Can I ask you something?"

"Anything." He could hear her exhaustion when she spoke.

"Can we not have sex again until this weekend?" Adrian thought about what she'd asked for a few minutes then broke into laughter. "Sure, baby." He rubbed her back and snuggled closer and deeper under the covers. "I can do that."

"Good." She sighed. "'Cause I'm really sore."

A few more minutes went by before Adrian spoke. "I love you, Skyler," he whispered before letting sleep overtake him.

Chapter Ten

Adrian noticed that time flew by, and with that time, he and Skyler got along well, Dedrick was still gloomy, and Sidney started to show with her pregnancy rather fast, which had to do with her having twins. Natasha worked hard with Sidney on the nursery, and Stefan became a nervous wreck. It seemed he needed to be everywhere that Sidney was to make sure she sat down, rested, and ate enough. Adrian loved teasing Stefan about being a mother hen, but deep down, he wished Skyler were carrying his child. Three cycles and heats had passed, yet she still wasn't pregnant, and it kind of bothered him. The further along Sidney became, the more Adrian dreamed.

"No way are you hanging that in here," Skyler told Adrian, her hands on her slim hips as he stood on the bed trying to hang a framed poster of a man looking half-dead.

Adrian got the poster on the nail and backed up to get a better look at it. He glanced over his shoulder at Skyler. "It's Marilyn Manson. I went to his concert."

"I don't care." She snickered. "You're not hanging it over *my* bed!"

Adrian jumped from the bed, cocked his head to one side, and crossed his arms over his chest. "*Your* bed?"

Skyler smiled and swayed on her feet. "Yeah, *my* bed." She dragged out the word *my* and took a step back.

"So, what happened to *ours* then?" He took a step closer with a grin, and she took a step back giggling.

"That was before you were going to hang crap like that in here." She pointed to the poster and laughed. "This room was decorated by a professional, Adrian. You can't trash it with shit like that."

"Shit!" Adrian placed his hand over his heart as if she had wounded him. "I have no shit. It's art."

"Ha!" She giggled.

"Oh, Skyler," Adrian called, lowering his hand and trying hard to act casual. "You are really asking for it."

"What I would be asking for is the fashion police to arrest me if I let that shit stay on my wall."

She screamed when he lunged at her. Adrian grabbed a hold of Skyler and started tickling her. "Take it back!"

"Never!" She laughed, fighting to get out of his hold. "It looks terrible and should be burned!"

"Hey." Stefan knocked on the open door, but didn't come inside.

As soon as Adrian saw him, he stopped tickling Skyler but kept his hold on her. "What's up?"

"Have you seen Sid?" Worry lines creased his face.

"Not since this morning," Skyler answered, wiggling out of Adrian's arms.

"Damn," Stefan groaned

"What's wrong?" Adrian asked again.

Stefan looked at Skyler, who nodded. "I get it. A male bonding moment is coming on." She turned and kissed Adrian quickly. "Take it down," she ordered under her breath with a push to his chest. "I'll go see if I can find her," she said to Stefan.

Adrian waited until Skyler was out of the room before he spoke again. "Give. What's going on?"

"Two things that aren't going to make my mate a very happy woman." Stefan sighed. One hand went to his hip, and he rubbed his face with the other. "Jaclyn called and isn't going to be coming back like she promised. She wouldn't say why, either. Sidney was looking forward to her coming."

Both hands went to his face, and then Stefan rubbed the back of his neck. That was a very bad sign. Stefan didn't get stressed out. He had a carefree and fun personality. He enjoyed teasing people, playing around, and enjoying life.

"Why is my gut telling me that I'm not going to like hearing what you've got to say next?" Adrian remarked, frowning.

"I also got a call from Dedrick. Sidney's father has moved, and we don't know where."

"When you say moved, you mean he just went on a vacation kind of move, right?" Adrian hoped like hell that is what it meant, but he knew it wasn't, and not because of Stefan shaking his head.

"The house is closed up," Stefan said. "Dedrick said there are boards on the windows. He thinks his operation has been moved, and if we don't know where he's at…"

"Then he could attack without us being prepared," Adrian finished. "Fuck!" the word exploded from his lips.

"Look." Stefan sighed. "I don't want Sid to know about her dad, not right now. At her last checkup, the doctor said her blood pressure was slightly up, and she didn't want her stressed out. It's bad enough that I'm going to have to tell her about Jaclyn not coming, but as far as her father, we keep this to ourselves."

Adrian nodded in agreement. "Yeah, we don't need her to worry over that."

Stefan also nodded, turned, but stopped. "I'm glad you and Skyler are getting along. I like seeing my baby sister happy."

Adrian smiled. "I feel so complete with her."

"I know the feeling." Stefan nodded again. "Okay, I'm off to find Sid to tell her about Jaclyn." He shook his head. "She's going to give me hell for not forcing Jaclyn to come anyway."

Adrian peered back at the poster and grinned before stepping back up on the bed and taking it down. Skyler did have a point. It didn't go with the rest of the décor. He left the room, hands in pockets, and walked down the hall, stopping at the nursery where he found Sidney. "Hey, Stefan's looking for you."

He took a couple steps closer and looked around the room. "Still no crib?" Adrian leaned against the door frame of the new nursery.

Sidney stood in the middle of the room, her hands on her hips, gawking around. The room didn't have much furniture yet. There were two changing tables, clothes that were neutral colors of whites and yellows, two rockers, and some baby toys. Everything, it seemed, but cribs.

"No." Sidney sighed. She went over to one of the rockers, sat down, and put her feet up on a matching footstool. She was about five months along, but it seemed like seven. "Natasha picked one out, but I didn't like it, and she didn't like mine, so we left mad. I feel guilty, but at the same time, I would love to have something in here that I picked out." She rubbed her belly. "Natasha is so excited and worried, too. She thinks she is doing me a favor, but she isn't. I want to enjoy this as well, you know?" She jumped and smiled. "They're kicking again. Anyway, I don't want to hurt her feelings, and I do appreciate what she's trying to do, but if Stefan doesn't get her to back off and let me take some charge of my kids' room, I swear I'm going to kill him."

She took a deep breath, closing her eyes for a few seconds before looking at him again. "Let me guess, Jaclyn called, and she isn't coming back yet."

"You're good." Adrian laughed. "And it's Natasha's way. She has been a single parent raising three kids for a long time. I'm sure if you talk to Stefan, he will get her to tone it down some."

"He better," Sidney stated. "Or I'm going to show him another meaning of the term pissed off, and I know Jaclyn."

Adrian glanced around the room thinking about how he and Skyler needed to get out, and it couldn't hurt for Stefan to take Sidney out, either. "Well, why don't we go shopping then?" He shrugged. "We could go out and get a bite to eat. Dedrick can entertain Natasha for a while, and the four of us could get out of the house."

Sidney seemed to light up. "You would go baby shopping?"

He saw the hope in her eyes and smiled. "Just shopping, not a life sentence. One day I hope to have some kids running around. We all need a break anyway, and there is this new restaurant I'm dying to try."

"What is it about you guys and food?" She extended her hand to him, and Adrian went over to help her up.

"Oh, I give you a few more weeks and you'll start eating everything in sight." He helped her to her feet. "You have half-shifters in there. Two of them, and if they're male, you'll be eating us out of house and home very soon."

"God, I hope I have girls then." Sidney snorted. "I already have the stretch marks from hell."

"So you still don't know what you're having?" Adrian followed Sidney out of the nursery and down the hall to her room where they stopped.

"No." She sighed. "Every time we go for the sonogram they turn so you can't tell. I swear, if I didn't know better, I would think they do it on purpose."

"They could be." Adrian smiled. "They could be strong-minded, and if they are, they could know what their mother is thinking or trying to do. The young of our kind are very mischievous, even in the womb. They have a very good chance of being able to slip into people's minds without them even knowing it. Call it a survival instinct. They are vulnerable and connected to you. I bet they know everything that is going on around you." He patted her on the shoulder. "Hate to break it to you, Sid, but shifter babes are damn smart, so you better get yourself all ready, or these two are going to pull a lot of shit on you." His smile got larger, letting his teeth show. "After all, they do have Stefan for a father, and he was not a piece of cake."

"Did I hear my name?" Stefan strolled up to them, grinning.

"Damn." Adrian smirked. "I'm never going to steal you away from him if he keeps popping up."

"If my sister hears that, your nuts are toast." Stefan teased back.

"We're going out," Sidney said. She smiled like a little girl who was getting a special treat.

"We are?" Stefan raised one eyebrow.

"We all need to get out," Adrian put in, leaning back against the wall, crossing his arms over his chest. "She needs a couple of cribs, and I want to try this new place, so the four of us are going out." He shrugged. "How simple can that be?"

"But dinner first," Sidney pointed out, her finger going up in the air.

"Yes, ma'am." Stefan got all serious, straightening his back and shoulders and looking like he was about to give her a salute.

Adrian laughed. "Okay, we meet outside in a couple of hours then?"

Stefan looked at Sidney, and Adrian saw the twinkle in his friend's eye. "Make it three." He started to wrestle with Sidney who was giggling.

"Two, Adrian," Sidney called out when Adrian pushed away from the wall and headed down to Skyler's room. "He isn't going to get what he thinks he is."

Adrian smiled, shook his head, and left the two of them alone. He walked into the bedroom just as Skyler came out wearing an open robe and one of the sexiest set of panties and bra he had seen in a long time. The set was black lace with thin straps over her shoulders and around her hips with a thin V strip covering her mound. Adrian's mouth watered at the sight, and quickly, he closed and locked the door. In an instant, he was hard and ready. He followed her into the closet and came up behind her as she was flipping through her clothes. He wrapped his arms around her waist, his lips going right for her neck as he moved one hand down her stomach to slip inside her panties.

"Adrian!" Skyler gasped. "I'm trying to get dressed."

"And I'm trying to undress you." He pulled back only enough to pull the robe from her shoulders. With his hand still inside her panties, Adrian turned her to the back of the closet where he had her plant her hands on the wall, her wide feet apart. "God, you're hot." Fighting with his jeans, he groaned when the button wouldn't open.

"In here!" she gasped when he plunged a finger inside her slick pussy.

"Right here." He jerked his jeans open, freeing his throbbing cock. "Right now." Adrian moved her panties to the side and positioned his cock. One sharp thrust with his hips, and he was buried balls deep inside her snug pussy with a moan. "Fuck, you're tight." He kissed her neck, licked up to her ear as he moved his hips savagely.

His hand stayed between her legs, parting the swollen lips of her pussy to play with the hard nub of her clit. With his other hand, he squeezed hard on one of her breasts, still covered in lace. Skyler moaned, arched her back, and moved against him.

"Yeah, baby." Adrian moaned, licking his mark on her shoulder. "Push back. Show me what you want."

Skyler's arms came up over her head, fingers linking into his hair. Adrian kept pounding into her, his climax approaching quickly. He moved his finger faster over her clit as he kneaded her breast.

"Shit, Adrian. God, fuck, it's coming."

Adrian gave her clit a pinch, and it was over. Skyler cried out, her pussy contracting hard around his cock. He bit down on the mark he had made on her shoulder the same second his cock erupted, spilling his thick seed deep into her. Moaning against her, he moved his cock to bring each and every drop of pleasure from their bodies he could.

"Damn it, Adrian." Skyler groaned. "Now I'm going to have to take another shower."

Adrian smiled and rested his head on her shoulder. "Well, if you do, don't let me see you come out in sexy panties again." He flicked her clit, which brought a whimper from her. "Or we might have to do this again."

"You are insatiable," she snorted and pushed him away from her.

"Only where you're concerned, babe." Smiling, he fixed his jeans. "Hey, we're going out with your brother and Sidney," he yelled while walking out of the closet to drop on the bed.

"You mean you can keep it in your pants that long?" she said sweetly over her shoulder.

"It'll be hard all night long." Adrian grinned. "I mean my dick, not keeping it in my pants."

"You're a perv." Skyler laughed and shook her head. "So what are we doing?"

"Dinner and some baby shopping." He heard the water start, and his cock rose. "Damn." He mumbled, sitting up in bed. "Here we go again."

Adrian stripped and rushed into the bathroom. Skyler screamed when he joined her, and her normal ten-minute shower lasted almost an hour with Adrian once again bending Skyler over and making love to her rough and fast.

* * * *

Like Stefan had said, Sidney, Skyler, Adrian, and Stefan left the house three hours later. The place that Adrian had wanted to try for dinner was a brand new steak and seafood restaurant. Stefan and Adrian ordered tons of food, some of which Sidney said she had never tasted and Skyler only wrinkled her nose at.

There were oysters, crab cakes, cheese sticks, and some kind of dip with chips. Salads came with their meals, and the guys had Sidney looking at them both like they were crazy by ordering both thick steaks and lobster. Skyler only ordered the steak. When the meal was finished, Sidney ordered one large slice of chocolate cake. She ate it all by herself with Stefan only getting the occasional stolen bite. Adrian enjoyed teasing her about it. Nothing was left to take home.

With stuffed bellies, the four went into a baby store. Right away

Stefan talked to a manager to set up delivery for anything that Sidney might pick out. As soon as that was finished, both Sidney and Skyler went off in search of cribs.

"I'm glad you two are getting along," Stefan said once the girls were far enough away and couldn't overhear. "She's happy again."

Adrian looked over at Skyler who was smiling at Sidney over a baby blanket. "You never know how empty your life is until you have that one special person."

"Tell me about it." Stefan chuckled. "And look at you, all soft on me."

Adrian chuckled. "You got soft way before me."

Stefan smiled, but it quickly went away. "She's my world, Adrian. I can't let anything happen to her."

"Nothing will," Adrian assured him. "She's part of my family now, and just like Skyler, I would give my life for Sidney if need be."

"Thanks." Stefan grinned. "Now who is going to save my bank account?" He frowned. "Sidney!"

Adrian laughed. All of their lives, the girls, hoping to impress, had flocked around Stefan and him. Sure, they had had their pick, but it soon became boring to have a girl around who only wanted to do what you wanted, who never stood up for herself. The last girl Adrian had dated had felt like a doll on his arm. She had always gone along with whatever he wanted, never saying what she wanted. It became very clear to Adrian after a few weeks that she was afraid to be herself, and her friends told him later on she hadn't wanted him to dump her so she went along with him. For that reason he stopped seeing her and stopped dating girls like her. Never had it dawned on any of the girls that what Adrian wanted the most was someone who not only stood up to him, but who also stood with him—a partner not a trophy.

"Come on, please!" Sidney begged Stefan. Adrian strolled up to the two, standing next to a crib. "It isn't that much."

"No, but it's two of them." Stefan pointed out. "And you want the stroller *and* car seats."

"Hey, where's Skyler?" Adrian asked.

"She went over there." Sidney pointed behind her back. "Said she saw something that she needed to take care of."

"In a baby store?" Adrian frowned and left Sidney and Stefan to debate over the crib. Adrian knew that Sidney was going to end up going home with what she wanted, even if Stefan didn't know it yet.

Adrian turned a corner and his gut dropped. Skyler was talking to Thomas Fallen again. It seemed like whatever she was telling him wasn't going over very well. In fact, Thomas looked downright pissed off, and that had Adrian worried that something bad was going to happen.

"Skyler," he called, startling Thomas.

When Adrian's gaze met Thomas's, Adrian knew then that it wasn't good. The man's eyes were wild, almost crazed, and he was stiff, almost like he was about to do something or move fast.

"Skyler, move!" Adrian yelled.

Skyler turned to face Adrian, but it was too late. She didn't move fast enough. Thomas moved quickly, clamping his arm around Skyler's neck. Slamming her back against his chest, he pulled out a gun, which he pointed at the side of her head.

"Back the fuck off," Thomas growled at Adrian.

Someone screamed, and Adrian skidded to a stop, his hands going up to show that he wasn't a threat to Thomas—yet, but it seemed that the scream made Thomas nervous.

"Thomas, what are you doing?" Adrian asked, keeping his voice calm.

"What the fuck do you think I'm doing?" he snarled, his eyes darkening with hate, his lip going up in a grimace. "I'm taking your mate, just like you took mine."

Adrian frowned. "I didn't take your mate."

Thomas backed up, dragging Skyler with him, and someone yelled to call the cops. People ran in all directions to get away from the nut holding a gun in the store, but Adrian didn't look at them. He only saw them from the corner of his eye. His attention was fixed on Skyler, who appeared so helpless it tore at his soul and broke his heart.

"Oh, yes you did." Thomas spat back, hate coming off him in waves. "Khiana. You remember her, don't you? I'm sure Skyler does." When all Adrian did was frown, Thomas laughed and backed up to the door. Shoppers were down on the ground holding their hands over their heads and whimpering as they moved out of his way "The girl you fucked in the woods at Stefan's wedding!" he yelled, which made a woman behind him cry out.

Adrian was starting to wonder where the fuck the cops were. How long would it be before someone attempted to play hero and tried to take Thomas out. Adrian didn't know how long he could keep Thomas here before the guy tried something that would hurt Skyler. From the corner of his eye, Adrian saw Stefan slowly trying to make his way behind Thomas, and fearing what would happen if Thomas saw him, Adrian gave a short, soft shake of his head.

"Skyler wasn't the only one to interrupt the two of you. I saw it all as well!" He yanked Skyler outside, and Adrian followed. "I watched you fuck my mate without a care in the world, never thinking about who you might hurt!"

"She wasn't mated," Adrian said levelly. A tear slipped from Skyler's eye as she stared at him. Off in the distance, he could hear the sweet sound of a siren. The cops were coming. He just needed to keep Thomas talking.

"She was promised to me," Thomas growled. "And you fucked that up." He sounded like he might cry, but didn't. Instead, he walked backwards until he got Skyler to a car parked on the side of the street. "It's not right for you to get everything you want while you ruin other people's lives." Thomas spoke calmly then, causing Adrian to worry. "So I'm going to stop you from hurting anyone else." He aimed the gun at Adrian.

Adrian thought his life was over. Everything was in slow motion, and he thought that what he was seeing was something from a movie. Flashes of his time growing up in the Draeger house hit. He saw himself teasing Skyler, and then giving her some ice cream when she was crying. He saw himself standing with his father at his mother's gravesite, could almost feel the tears falling down his cheeks, and then the memory shifted to the day he buried his father. Natasha held his hand, giving him the comfort that he needed. The last memory that shot into his brain was the night he had sex with Khiana in the woods. The truces, the love, all of it hit him when he looked at the gun pointed at his chest.

"Time to say good night." Thomas smiled.

"No!" Skyler screamed.

Just before the gun went off, she lunged after it, pushing Thomas's arm to the side. The bullet didn't hit his chest or stomach like Adrian thought it would, but it tore into his shoulder, knocking him hard to the ground.

"Adrian!" Skyler screamed. "Adrian!"

Adrian glanced up to see Thomas hit Skyler hard on the side of her head, and then shove her into the backseat of the car. His head was spinning with pain, and he felt like he couldn't move. Blood poured out of the wound, spilling onto the sidewalk as Thomas got into the car and started it.

Adrian managed to roll over and come to his knees, using one arm to push himself up. "Skyler," he mumbled, head hanging as he fought the dizziness and the weakness quickly taking over. When he forced himself to look up, the car was pulling away. "Skyler!" he bellowed right before the car took off with a screech.

"Son of a bitch!" Stefan rushed up to him and held onto Adrian's shoulders to prevent him from falling face down on the sidewalk. "That motherfucker shot you!"

Sidney also rushed up, going down to her knees before him, taking hold of his head. Sweat was on his face, plastering his hair to his forehead, and Adrian felt as if he was going to pass out. In fact, he knew he was. He had to shake his head against the pain and the blackness that was starting to close around him. In his head, he also heard a siren that was getting closer and closer.

"Stefan, the cops!" Sidney said. Her voice sounded muffled to Adrian as he fought the blackness in his head.

"Thomas," he panted, looking up at Stefan. "Thomas...has...her," he managed to get out before the darkness wrapped its arms around him.

* * * *

"Well, the Council isn't going to help," Dedrick announced, his hands on his hips, glaring around the room. He was beyond pissed off and knew his body language was showing it. "They are suggesting we do this with the old laws."

Natasha snorted, which surprised Dedrick because it wasn't something she did. "They are nothing short of barbaric animals." She stood up and started to pace her sitting room. "Everything to those animals is said and done with violence. It's a damn wonder we all have made it this long with them."

"Yeah, well, Thomas made a claim on Skyler about a month after Adrian, behind my back!" Dedrick jabbed a finger in his own chest. "The little fucker," he snarled. "So Adrian is going to have to fight for her."

Stefan shook his head and growled low. "He was shot with copper," he said to Dedrick and Natasha. Sidney was upstairs with Adrian to make sure he didn't start bleeding again. After they brought him into the house, Dedrick had gone to work at digging out the bullet before more damage could be done. Since Thomas used a copper round, if left inside, an infection could take hold in his blood, and Adrian would die. All shifters were allergic to copper, not silver like the folk tales. "There is no damn way he can fight Thomas."

"I don't want my daughter with that man!" Natasha yelled. She gave Dedrick one of her looks that had him taking a step back.

"What would you have me do?" Dedrick asked, fighting to keep his voice level out of respect that his mother deserved. "Two men have placed a claim on her, and by our law, they have to fight it out." He growled, rubbing his eyes to stop the headache that threatened to come. "It's too late to demand a dissolve, but Thomas does have the right to challenge Adrian's claim."

"Barbaric," Natasha said again, shaking her head.

"He's right." Adrian stood in the doorway, or more like leaned against the door. Sidney was on his other side trying to hold him up. "It's my fight."

Dedrick looked at Adrian. He was pale, with dark circles around his eyes, and the bandage over the gun wound that went from front to back was soaked in blood. He also had his arm in a sling.

If that copper bullet had been shot into Adrian's chest or stomach, it would have killed him. Dedrick knew Adrian was damn lucky it only hit his shoulder, but still it was doing a number on him—it wouldn't stop bleeding right away, and with each drop of blood he lost, precious energy was also lost.

"You can't go," Dedrick said. "Plain and simple." He finished with a bark. "I'm going to go."

"Dedrick!" Natasha cried.

"I'm the head of the family," Dedrick growled. "It's my responsibility!"

Natasha rushed up to him, taking hold of his face. Stefan went to help Adrian sit down. "Not everything is yours to take care of," she told Dedrick, in a way that was calm and soothing. It seemed to do the trick, because Dedrick felt himself calm down. She smiled, before kissing him on the cheek. "Now," she turned to the group, "we need to think about what we're going to do in order to bring Skyler home."

"I'm going to go and bring her home," Adrian said.

"I don't think you're going to get far, buddy." Stefan grinned. "You kind of look like shit."

Adrian gave a tired smile before he flipped Stefan off.

"Time isn't on our side." Dedrick crossed his arms over his chest and fixed his eyes on Adrian. "Thomas has already made the call it seems before you ran into him at the store. He wants your claim dissolved. With my call to the Council that gives us at least forty-eight hours for you to protect your claim on Skyler or fight for her before the Council steps in and decides for us." Dedrick rubbed his face, feeling like an old man, which he wasn't. He rubbed the back of his neck and paced the floor a few times before stopping in front of Adrian. "So you have one day to get your ass in gear and go kick his."

"And what are you going to do?" Adrian groaned, shifting in his seat.

"I'm going to try and stall." Dedrick sighed. "But I have no clue how yet."

Silence greeted the room as everyone thought about what would help them get Skyler home safely. Sidney finally broke the silence, halting Dedrick's pacing in the center of the room with a question.

"Does he have a weakness for hot girls?"

Dedrick frowned, apparently not understanding how that question could help any of them any more than Adrian did. "Sure." He shrugged. "Who wouldn't?"

Sidney smiled, and Dedrick suddenly knew where this train of thought was going. "I don't think that would be the best idea."

"Um, would you two like to clue the rest of us in, please?" Natasha said.

Dedrick said nothing as Sidney turned and smiled at her mother-in-law. "You need a way to get to Thomas, and I think I know the perfect person who can give you the right kind of distraction."

"No way," Stefan cried. "You can't bring Jaclyn into this, Sidney. She's human!"

"So am I!" Sidney yelled back. "Look, she can help distract this guy for Adrian."

"Come on, Sid." Dedrick sighed. "Stefan has a point. You don't want to bring her into the middle of a shifter battle."

"Fine." Sidney shrugged. "Then you come up with something else."

"Sidney's right," Natasha finally said. "As much as I hate to do this, I think Jaclyn would be able to help here."

"Ma..." Dedrick groaned.

"Thomas looks at himself as the kind of male who helps people," Natasha went on. "I believe he thinks that he's helping Skyler. He hasn't seen Jaclyn, so that alone gives us an edge I think will be very helpful."

Dedrick groaned. "But she's human."

"That has nothing to do with this," Natasha snapped. "If she can make Thomas think she needs help . . ."

"Then his guard is down," Adrian finished with a knowing smile. "I like it."

Stefan chuckled. "How about the simple, 'My car broke down. Can you help me?' A guy like Thomas won't be able to say no if we get Jaclyn looking hot as hell." Sidney elbowed Stefan in the gut, and Adrian chuckled.

Dedrick hated to admit it, but they all did have a point. He didn't know Thomas that well, but knew that the guy had a hero complex going on. Thomas Fallen couldn't say no to a knock down gorgeous woman asking for help. As crazy as it all sounded, he did think it would work to get the man outside where Adrian could take him on.

"You all are nuts," Dedrick finally said, rubbing the back of his neck. "Fine." He shrugged again, shoved his hands into his jean pockets, and glared at Stefan. "Call her then."

Sidney smiled at Dedrick, and then looked at Stefan. "She hangs out at Martinis."

"Then I guess Martinis is where I'm going." Stefan sighed and sat back.

Chapter Eleven

"You two are out of your minds!" Sidney cried, tossing her arms up in the air. She paced the floor in Dedrick's office while he leaned against the front of the desk and Jaclyn lounged in one of his leather chairs. "You can't go out like that," she said to Jaclyn.

"This was your idea," Stefan reminded her, which got him a dirty look.

"You said change into something hot," Jaclyn said. "Stefan said it was hot."

Jaclyn was dressed in a very short jean skirt that was cut from a pair of blue jeans, a leather tank top that in Sidney's eyes should have been *over* a shirt or something, not worn *as* a shirt. She wore a pair of cowboy boots, and her long hair hung loose. As much as Sidney hated to admit it, if that outfit couldn't get Thomas out of the house, then nothing would. Jaclyn was hot!

"Thomas will be fooled," Dedrick said evenly, his arms crossed over his chest. "He can't resist pretty girls."

"Ah, you think I'm pretty," Jaclyn sang, placing her hand over her heart. "That's so touching."

Dedrick gave her a dirty glare before he went on. "Besides, like Stefan said, this was your idea. She does her flirty shit, gets him out the door. That's it. From there we can do the rest."

Sidney sighed. "You guys have her dressed like a piece of meat."

"And I'll stop him before he eats her up," Dedrick said. "Don't worry. Stress isn't good for you or them." He pointed to her belly.

"Chill, Sid. I'll help out, get Skyler back home, and then everyone can go back to being one big happy family." Jaclyn stood and smiled at Dedrick. "Maybe I should change, for her." She nodded toward Sidney.

She started to walk out, but Dedrick stopped her. "No. Wear that." He worked hard at keeping his expression normal and not let it get heated or out of control. "It will work fine for Thomas."

Jaclyn smiled up at him. "Okay. You're the boss." She looked over at Sidney. "Don't worry so much. It'll be a piece of cake." She kissed Sidney on the cheek, then turned back to Dedrick, and winked before she left the room.

"You know." Sidney strolled over to Dedrick, her eyes narrowed on him. "There is something going on between you two. I don't know what it is, but you had better make sure it doesn't hurt her. Jaclyn has been hurt too many times, and I'm not going to see it happen again."

"I'm not going to hurt her," Dedrick said. "I promise to stay as far away from her as I can, and nothing is going on."

Sidney nodded. "Protect her out there."

Dedrick smiled. "I will protect her with my life. Now will you go up and check on Adrian while I take care of the other stuff?"

"What the hell did I get myself into when I married this family?" she mumbled, walking out of the office.

*****

"Are you sure this is going to work?" Adrian asked Dedrick for about the tenth time. They watched Jaclyn stroll up the drive to Thomas's house, swaying her hips seductively. "I can't see Thomas straying so soon after he has Skyler underfoot."

Dedrick grinned, and it sent a chill down Adrian's spine. "Oh, it will work." His eyes were on Jaclyn, and once again, they fixed on her ass.

Adrian started to wonder what was going on with the man where Jaclyn was concerned. Since Jaclyn had come back to the house, Adrian had noticed that Dedrick seemed tense. "Okay, man, I've got to ask this." Adrian took a deep breath before he turned toward Dedrick. "What the hell is going on with you?" When Dedrick frowned, Adrian quickly went on. "The moment Jaclyn walked into the house you became all alpha and shit. I know you said that you were feeling something a while ago, but is it changing?"

Dedrick held onto the steering wheel so tight his knuckles started to turn white. "I don't know what's going on." Dedrick sounded on the edge, like he was fighting for control.

"I think you do, man."

Dedrick looked at Adrian quickly, and Adrian was able to see the slight flash of red in his eyes, even though he said, "I'm fine."

"Dedrick, it's not the end of the world if you end up mated to a human. Your brother is, and they're doing fine."

"Can we talk about something else?" Dedrick growled.

Adrian nodded and turned back to the front. A few minutes went by before Dedrick spoke again, and Adrian was pretty sure Dedrick had allowed the silence to stretch just to get him pissed off. It worked.

"I'm sure Thomas is ready to get laid big time, and I would bet my last dollar Skyler is feeling anything but loveable." Dedrick chuckled. "After I saw firsthand how my sister brought you down to your knees with one kick, I sort of feel sorry for Thomas." He held up his hand, pinching two fingers together. "About that much, though."

The thought of Thomas trying anything with Skyler had Adrian growling. The only man who was going to be touching her was him! "He touches her and I'm going to rip his mother-fucking throat out!"

Dedrick chuckled. He opened the driver's side door. "Come on. If Jaclyn gets hurt, Sidney will have *my* nuts."

"He's going to pick up our scents," Adrian said through gritted teeth, trying to keep his voice low.

"We're not going up to the fucking house," Dedrick growled back, glaring over his shoulder at Adrian. "She's going to bring him out to us and with no wind we have the upper hand."

"That's your great plan!" Adrian worked hard to stay quiet, but it was difficult. "Remind me again why I brought you and not Stefan," he finished sarcastically.

"Stop whining," Dedrick growled.

They stopped at the end of the drive, hid behind some bushes and waited. Adrian could feel the excitement rushing in his veins and the need for some kind of violence hit. He wanted to hurt Thomas so bad he could almost taste the blood.

"This isn't going to work," Adrian whispered.

"Yes it is, now shut the fuck up," Dedrick snapped back.

Five minutes went by, and they'd not seen hide nor hair of Jaclyn until suddenly she came walking down the drive with Thomas on her arm. She was all smiles and laughing as Thomas talked, and Adrian felt

Dedrick tense up. When he looked at Dedrick, he saw a hint of red in his eyes and thought he heard a low growl.

"Where did you say your car was?" Thomas asked Jaclyn.

"Right around here." She smiled back. "I swear the damn thing is always breaking down on me."

Dedrick moved first, and Adrian followed. They waited until they could jump behind Thomas, catching him completely off guard. It worked. By the time Thomas picked up on them both, Dedrick and Adrian were standing behind him.

Thomas stopped and peeked over his shoulder. Jaclyn slowly backed away from him, and he lunged at her, but Jaclyn managed to jump back and kick him so hard in the nuts that Thomas went down to his knees holding his crotch.

"Pick on someone your own size," she spat at him before turning and running back up to the house.

"So what now?" Thomas groaned. He struggled to get back up to his feet to face Adrian who was growling softly.

"Now, I'm going to kick your ass," Adrian snapped. "Then I'm going to take my mate back home."

Thomas laughed. "She's mine!" he yelled. "I took her, and I'm placing *my* claim on her."

"She already has a mark." Adrian smirked back. "Mine!"

Both changed into their wolf forms at the same time, their clothes ripping as their bodies became larger. Adrian was a good foot taller than Thomas, but Thomas had a wider build, so they were matched fairly. Adrian lunged first, swiping wide with his paw but catching nothing but air. Thomas, however, managed to make contact with Adrian's side.

Dedrick didn't move, only stood in the middle of the driveway watching the scene.

"What the hell is going on?" Jaclyn demanded, standing next to Dedrick.

"A fight," he said. "What's it look like?"

"Dedrick!" Skyler rushed up to him, but when she made a move toward Adrian, Dedrick grabbed her and stopped her from going any farther. "Stop this!"

Adrian heard her voice and howled. His mate was free, but the fight for the dominance was still at hand. Adrian was going to show Thomas that one didn't take another's mate without consequences. Only when he brought Thomas down would he prove the point that Skyler was his!

Thomas charged him, and Adrian knew then it was all over. He moved with grace and skill, turning to the right and swinging his thick arm over his back to grab Thomas with his large paw around his throat. Adrian picked the man up and slammed him down to the ground with enough force that some of the concrete cracked.

Holding Thomas down by his throat, just like that, Adrian cut off enough of his air to force Thomas to change back into his human form. Once he did, Adrian, panting hard from the adrenaline, also changed back.

"I should kill you for what you've done," Adrian said, fighting the instinct to squeeze the life from him.

"What about what you've done?" Thomas squeaked, holding onto Adrian's arm with both hands. "You ruined my life."

"I didn't ruin your life!" Adrian growled. "Khiana is still there for you." He gave him a hard jerk before letting go. Adrian slowly stood up, keeping his eyes on Thomas. "I'm going to let you live, only because killing you will do nothing but cause me shit with my mate, but I swear if you try this shit again, I will rip your fucking throat out without even blinking." He growled again. "Understand?"

Thomas only nodded. Adrian looked up and smiled when he saw Skyler staring back at him. He moved fast, rushing toward her as she ran to him. When they met, he wrapped her tightly in his arms.

"Are you all right?" he asked, resting a hand at the back of her head and the other one at her waist. She nodded and matched his bear hug. "God, I love you, Skyler." He moaned, closing his eyes and feeling like the world was slowly crashing down on his shoulders.

Skyler seemed to burrow herself into him. "I'm sorry," she whispered. "I'm sorry for everything."

"You have nothing to be sorry for," he told her.

"Yes, I do." She pulled back slightly to look him in the eye. "I'm sorry I didn't tell you earlier that I do love you." She smiled, and a tear fell. "I have since I was a little girl, Adrian."

He smiled. "Well, it's about time you admit it. I was starting to wonder when you'd realize it," he finished with a chuckle.

"Well, this is nice and cozy." Jaclyn said, smiling when Adrian peered up at her. "But it would be better if you had some clothes on."

Skyler pulled out of his arms and glanced down. She started to laugh, her eyes taking in the state of undress he was in. "Showing off my goods?" she asked him.

"Oh, well, you know." He shrugged. "When you've got it, why not flaunt it?"

Skyler grabbed his nipple and twisted it. Adrian cried, "Not funny," and then laughed, but he stopped when he saw the bruise on the side of her face from where Thomas had hit her to get her into his car.

"Don't." She pushed his hand away. When her eyes came to rest on his shoulder, which had started to bleed again, she gasped. She reached out and caressed the wound. "God, you shouldn't even be fighting!" she cried softly.

"Well, now we can go home, and you can take care of me properly." He sighed. Adrian bowed his head, feeling the weight of the night's events hit him like a ton of bricks. "Dedrick, I think I'm going to need some help."

"No shit," Dedrick answered. "You look like hell."

* * * *

"So how's he doing?" Dedrick asked Stefan. Dedrick was leaning against the wall, dressed in clean jeans and a black T-shirt with his arms crossed over his chest.

"Better," Stefan answered with a sigh. "The copper is slowly leaving his system. That fight and change seemed to help get most of it out. He's weak, but will live."

Dedrick nodded. "And Skyler?"

"Happy as a little girl on Christmas morning." Stefan smiled. "Sidney is babying her until Mom is finished with Adrian."

Dedrick grunted. "Then everything is peachy again."

Stefan chuckled. "I don't think things are going to be peachy ever again, Dedrick. Too much excitement around here."

Dedrick nodded again. "Go to your wife, Stefan. It's been a long night."

Dedrick waited a few minutes before he pushed away from the wall and started down the stairs. He was halfway down when he saw Jaclyn walking to the front door with her bag slung over her shoulder.

"Running again?" he called, continuing his walk downstairs.

She stopped and twirled around on her heels. "I'm not running."

"So what would you call it?" He cocked his head to one side.

"A change of scenery." She smiled.

He snorted, stopping at the bottom step to lean against the banister. "Did you even bother to say good-bye to Sidney?"

"I left her a note."

"A note." One eyebrow went up and a mocking smile crossed his face. "That's sweet."

"Look." She pinched the bridge of her nose. "This here"—Jaclyn swung one arm wide—"is all nice and dandy, but it's not mine. She has a home, and I'm very happy for her. Sidney deserves to have a great family who loves her and is willing to take great care of her, but the family thing doesn't work for me." She took a deep breath, letting it out slowly. "Besides, you and me in the same room could get lethal."

"She thinks of you as family," he stated, ignoring her last statement. She was right, though, they were lethal together.

"Yeah, well, there's still nothing for me here." She made a tsk sound, swaying back and forth on her feet. "I have found that staying in one place for too long is never a good thing."

"You're running from something, Jaclyn, and one day, you're not going to be able to run from it any longer."

She seemed taken aback by what he said. "What, you think you know me now?"

"I run every month," Dedrick growled. "Look." He took a deep breath, letting it out slowly. "Sidney worries about you, and with her being pregnant, it isn't good for her or the babes."

She walked up to him, close, so close Dedrick felt his cock stir in his jeans. Slowly, like a dream, Jaclyn rose up on her toes and kissed him on the lips. Dedrick didn't fight it. In fact, he opened his mouth and kissed her back. He closed his eyes and sighed at the pleasure he felt from her lips pressed to his own, but as fast as it had started, it was over, and she was backing away from him.

"What was that for?" he asked softly, forcing his eyes to open.

"You're a good big brother for Sidney." She smiled. "You take care of everyone but you." Licking her lips, she backed to the door and pointed at him. "You need to look out for yourself once in a while." Jaclyn, keeping her eyes on him, opened the door. "I promised Sidney that I would be back for the birth." She rolled her eyes, acting very uncomfortable after the kiss. When he glared at her, Jaclyn quickly went on. "Look, I have got to go."

Dedrick saw she was angry and let it go. He was pissed off at himself for kissing her, pissed off at enjoying it, and pissed off that he made himself swear years ago not to fuck around with another human. Ultimately, he was pissed off that standing right in front of him was a human he suddenly wanted nothing more than to fuck. "Fine." He shrugged, giving her his best impression of 'I don't give a fuck what you do'. "You go run away. Seems that's the thing you do best."

Jaclyn gave him a dirty look. "That's the pot calling the fucking kettle black." The door slammed before he had a chance to say more to her.

* * * *

"So do we get to have another big wedding?" Sidney asked at breakfast the next morning, looking from Adrian to Skyler.

Skyler blushed, and Adrian chuckled.

"We really don't do that," Skyler said. When Sidney frowned, she went on. "Okay, shifters don't really do a wedding thing. See, when Adrian put his mark on my shoulder, that's pretty much the wedding, the ring, and everything."

"Then why did Stefan have our wedding?" Sidney frowned.

"Because you're human," Natasha answered.

"And you wanted it." Stefan grinned.

"So you don't get anything!" Sidney sat back in her chair and huffed. "That doesn't seem right."

Natasha smiled. "That's why we have these parties. We celebrate the joining of mates, births, and family."

"Well, if I don't get to do a big wedding or shower for you," Sidney said, sitting back up in the chair, "then I'm sure as hell going to buy you something."

Jaden Sinclair

"Oh, no." Stefan groaned. "More damn shopping."

* * * *

Conner Martin sat behind an old oak desk that was neat and clean with not one speck of dirt on it or one paper out of place. His cold gray eyes were fixed on a photo of a young Sidney, at about age ten, smiling. It was the only photo of her he had left. All the others he had destroyed the day he found out she was to marry that damn animal.

Conner was now in his late fifties, almost sixty, and his only child was practically dead to him. To Conner, he had an empire to give and needed to find someone who shared the same passion for this war he did.

He tapped his fingers on the desk, thinking about what his next move might be. Conner wasn't as young as he used to be, and all the scotch he drank didn't help, either. He was old, but the desire was still there to rid the world of these freaks.

As luck had it, Conner Martin did have someone who shared his passion. Josh Stan, Mike Stan's son. Since the night Mike was killed, Josh had picked up right where his father had left off. The perfect candidate to take over once Conner was gone.

Josh was close to Sidney's age, slightly older. He was the kind of man Conner would have loved for his daughter to marry. He felt it a waste that they weren't.

"My contact just sent these over." Josh came into the office with an air of authority that Conner loved. He didn't carry himself as a man too afraid to take what he wanted, just like him.

A brown folder was tossed onto his desk, and Conner tore his eyes away from the smiling little girl to it. He opened the folder and pulled out colored photos. All of them were of Sidney shopping. She was smiling, looking as if she was having the time of her life, but that wasn't what had Conner's full interest or his heart beat quickening. What had his attention was the roundness of her stomach.

He glanced up at Josh, who smiled. "Yes. She's pregnant. About four or five months along."

Conner said nothing. Looking back down at the pictures, he touched the smiling face of the daughter he no longer claimed. A child. She carried a child of one of those animals! Conner began to laugh. It was perfect! What better way to get the perfect specimen he needed for his next experiment?

"I want that child," Conner Martin stated in a chillingly flat voice.

* * * *

"So how many do you want?" Adrian and Skyler were lying in the bed cooling off from another intense lovemaking session. His arms were wrapped tightly around her, and her head rested on his chest.

Skyler giggled. "I don't know!"

"You must have some idea." Adrian rubbed his hand up and down her back. For the past ten minutes, he had been trying to get Skyler to think about how many kids she might want, and so far, she didn't have an answer for him. "What about six?"

She snorted, rising up on her elbows to look down at him. "You're out of your mind!"

Adrian chuckled. "Too many?"

"How about we just go with the flow and see what happens."

He frowned, bit the inside of his mouth, and tried to act like he was thinking about it before he nodded. "Agreed." Adrian pulled her back down to his chest and held her tight. "Besides, I like the practicing and need much, much more of it."

"Oh, please!" Skyler laughed and nudged him in the side.

"Skyler?"

She took a deep breath, letting it out slowly. "Hum?"

"I love you."

Kissing his chest, she snuggled closer. "I love you, too. Now will you please go to sleep? I'm exhausted."

With his arms tightly around his mate, Adrian smiled into the night. Finally, he was at peace with the one woman he loved with everything in his soul. As his eyes slowly closed, the last thought Adrian had made him smile. Once and for all, he had claimed Skyler for his own.

**Other works by Jaden Sinclair
at www.melange-books.com**

The Proposal

S.H.I.L.O.
S.E.T.H.

THE PLANETARY SERIES
Interplanetary Passion, Book 1
Outerplanetary Sensations, Book 2
Solar Seduction, Book 3

SHIFTER SERIES
Stefan's Mark
Claiming Skylar
Dedrick's Taming
The Prowling
Cole's Awakening
The New Breed
Seducing Sasha
Draeger's Legacy
Darian's Surrender
Full Moon Bites
Reluctant Heat
Unbounded Fury
Untamed Beast
Conquering Lyssa

Love at First Sight
Toy Soldier

Forbidden Tales Series
Tales of the Forbidden, Book 1, Forbidden Temptation
Tales of the Forbidden, Book 2, Forbidden Rapture
Tales of the Forbidden, Book 3, Forbidden Innocence
Tales of the Forbidden, Book 4, Forbidden Lust

Coming Soon!
Lord of Darkness

Lightning Source UK Ltd.
Milton Keynes UK
UKOW03f1313171216
290239UK00001B/233/P